Dance of Destinies

By Sandra Heavens

Table of Contents

MARIGOLD AND FRIENDS

Chapter 1
Marigold

When you're just a small seed, almost anything can happen to you. You can be buried and grow, blow away in the wind, be stomped on, trampled, or even drown in water. A seed can grow in almost any kind of condition, but with a little love and care, the result will amaze anyone.

As a seed, you have the potential to become anything you want. Once you're found, you're planted, nurtured, and loved. Being cared for is a part of growing, and being loved is the warmth that helps nurture growth.

Growing up, you want to be strong and beautiful and aspire to be the most beautiful flower with curling tendrils, trailing leaves, or spiky petals. But you must be just you!

I was dreaming of becoming alive. I wasn't sure at first if it was a feeling or just my imagination. Was I a seed that made the journey through the winter months? I would often wonder: "Am I living on my own, or do I feel so alone? I'm sure there are more of us, but I can't see or hear anything. I just want to be alive. That is my dream. It's so dark in here. I'm meant to be here for a reason, I can feel it."

I yearned to feel the warmth of the sun and be part of the flower families already blooming. I dreamt that maybe a gardener, a guardian of sorts, would nurture me to live a full, blooming life. I knew I wasn't the prettiest of flowers, and I came from an ordinary background. I once belonged to a loving family that stayed together in the flower world.

"Here we are," I thought. "Hundreds of seeds of all shapes and sizes, not knowing what or where we will end up. Here I am on some bench, and the smell of fertilizers and water is ever so strong. Perhaps if I uncover myself a little, someone will find me."

The days are long as there is little sun. Suddenly along comes a man. "I think he works here. Oh, yes, he's a Guardian of the plants. 'Pick me, pick me,'" I shout out loud, hoping that he will hear me.

The Guardian is sorting the varieties of plants and seeds. I am still laying on the bench, stuck in a flowerpot, with the hope of being found. The Guardian is continually sweeping the floor. If I fall, I don't know what will happen to me. I push myself further into the soil of the leftover dirt in this pot. The days grow longer, and the nights are just as long, when suddenly, out of nowhere, I feel I am being scooped up. Am I imagining this? I hope he sees me; oh, why did I push myself further into the dirt…oooooh. No, I am being planted in a little box. Guardian knows just the right amount of dirt I need to cover me. I think I have been found. I do hope all my other friends from last year are okay and get found and planted as well. Some of them may not be recognizable; others will bring themselves back to life with the help of Nature. It's up to me now; I am here on my own. Got to love that sunshine; It is so good on my top covers, helping me push my way to the top of the soil. Hope Guardian doesn't pick me as a weed. A butterfly has just crossed the path of the nursery, a great sign; the past flowers are with us in spirit. There she is visiting all us flowers…

I have cousin flowers, long-lost relative petals and seed friends that came to life. Some of them I have never met before. Most of the flowers that are alive are happy ones.

I couldn't help but think of the sad, lost seedlings along the way.

The Guardian of the nursery was making my every wish and dream come true.

Here it is, April, and the Guardian planted me! I was a small seed from my parents. They sadly passed away the previous fall. We all came from Mexico, but my family seedlings all migrated to other parts of North America to bring color and smiles to everyone around us. They came by cargo van where they saw little or no daylight, often for days, sometimes a week or more.

Migration sometimes was a seedling blowing in the wind, caught up in a bush and tumbling their way north. Having a stroke of luck, you could say, I was at the bottom of a planter that forgot to get washed out at the end of the growing season. You might say I'm the luckiest seed alive. The smallest seed ever, that's me. I was kept alive in a dark place until April, and here I am on the ground with many others that have had the same journey as I have. Kind of an orphan of the flower seeds that will grow up to be happy.

From the nursery bed, I was given lots of fresh air, loads of sunshine, love, and care. Cultivation was gentle. The sun's rays are still my favorite daytime friend; like the water, lots of water, I am always thirsty. Breaking out of the ground in June, I was born to be rugged and tough, a showy border kind of tough flower. The kind you will notice when you walk up the pathway. I am sturdy and bright yellow in color. Marigold is my name. I have made it. I am alive, a little plant waiting for the need to bloom, showing bright and showy in a garden.

Looking around the nursery, I saw so many relations.

You always get that one cousin who likes to outdo all the rest of us yellow and gold; Maroon Marigold, yup, that's

4

the one, she is very splashy if I do say so myself. She is one of many colors in our family. There are no seeds to pick from my petals. My dream is to live and share my beauty under the name 'Merry and Gold,' bringing smiles to all who look at me in the nursery or in a garden. Everyone needs a Marigold Garden, don't they? The Guardian has nurtured me to be healthy and able to live on my own. While here, I have met all sorts of great flowers. I've had my share of great conversations; I have learned a lot. I am Marigold, and this is my story. I am tiny and brown in color, and I have lots of little lines that go through my tiny little body. When I grow up, I will be a strong, green-leafed plant. Those will be my wings that will flutter in the breeze. I will have a bright, and I do mean bright yellow/gold/orange color to my body. My little petals will repel invasive nematodes, and I am deer resistant and very easy to grow. I love the sun, and I make a great companion to anyone's garden. I can tolerate the heat, and my friends love me as I grow in any kind of soil. I resemble a little daisy when I am full grown.

Chapter 2
Friends

I have so many friends. You can never have enough friends. Some of them, we meet along the way, some by chance, others by fate. This story is about the Love of Friends you meet along the way. Every friend has a story, and everyone has a friend to share their story to.

In the forest areas, there are all the wildflowers. Delicate Blue Bell is just one from the area. She is bell-shaped, with turned-up tips like she is stuck up, but far from it. They blow in the wind, so light and cheerful. Blue Bell often has a light purple touch to her waves. She claims it's all-natural in color. She loves to have white tips, ever so dainty, like a ballerina of flowers.

Blue Bell one told me, "I grow wild and wouldn't change my accommodations for anything. Sometimes I am a seed that is planted in an English Country Garden. Being well-travelled, my passport is full."

The Guardian, the man of the greenhouse, tried to keep us color-coordinated; the blue with the blue, red with red, you get my drift. I'm laughing as we tend to socialize and stay within our 'family name'. During the night, as we move about, we all find new places to stay for the night. The next morning, the guardian scratches his head when he comes and detects we are all over the place. This keeps life interesting. We all get a giggle. He seems to carry on his routine without hesitation.

Crocuses, they are always the first ones out of the ground, announcing it is spring. We often see our friend Crocus in the fields and rocky terrain. Sometimes you can find them in a garden; someone has a crocus bulb and planted them in the fall before the snow fell. They, too, will push the last remnants of snow away, showing they are ready to bloom. They announce to the rest of the flowers that it's time to dust yourself off and make your presence known.

Crocus also said me, "I come in white as well as blue. My center is yellow, and I love to live close to the ground." Unfortunately, the deer like to eat the crocus flower, so some are not around to tell their story.

Daisies also announce spring. They, too, have a colored center. They are from the Aster family and are quite innocent looking. You could say they came from a blended family. Blended families are good. They are happy. They make our gardens full of life and love.

Larkspurs are very hardy and, like me, Marigold, are quite splashy.

Larkspur said, "I grow tall as I can oversee what is going on." You know what she told me, "Well, I don't like to gossip, but Wild Rose is in town." Like Wild Rose, Larkspur doesn't drink a whole lot, she likes it on the dry side.

Then there is the Indian Paintbrush. They are a rich red color. Regal looks in the forest they call home. I stumbled across the Paintbrushes one day quite by accident, and they told me all about themselves. I am so jealous of what they have done too. The indigenous people used them to paint their bodies in the wild, which was so many years ago. The redder, the better. Like a war paint, the Indian red told of the past and present. You aren't allowed to pick them as they are very precious and endangered. People have picked them, and now we need to let them be in the wild so no one will ever forget them. Bright red, that's them. You can't miss them. Painter's paradise, for sure.

Even the trees have flowers when they are budding out in the spring. They love their new greenery to surprise everyone after a long winter. From the trees, acorns have dropped their seeds from above. Mother Nature's way of replenishing the forest. Nature has a way of awakening all of us after a long winter's nap. I have so many friends I have met along the way. Please, if you see any of them, tell them Marigold says hi.

When you are in such good care of the Guardian, you become acquainted with different families, and each one has its own story of history. Some do not like to talk too much, but, of course, in their own way, they are happy and beautiful. Some have a most delicate scent, and some have no smell at all. We are all pretty to see. Some of us are tall, I am short, but I love to look up to others, some even would like to look down at you. They watch over us shorter ones and let us know if any danger prevails. Long and tall, short and stout, we all have our looks that make us individuals.

Lilacs are some of my favorite May friends. They are very woody looking and strong. These lilacs attract hummingbirds and butterflies, who do love the sweet nectar in their blossom. They will grow so tall and so bushy. Smaller is nice too. The sweet scent of their delicate petals leaves you yearning for more. The colors are usually lavender, sometimes white and sometimes pink, but their smell is all the same.

One time, Lilac told me, "People love my Springtime smell after the long winter. They often will cut my branches for vases inside their homes. The only thing is, you need to change my water in the vase quite regularly, or it can cause quite a stink. When people see me, they know it is May and summer is just around the corner. Early to bed, early to rise, that is my life."

A good old friend is Dahlia.

She says, "I am a warm-weather friend."

But aren't we all? I say to myself, laughing.

Coming out in August, she really is the pride of her family. Dahlia also comes from Mexico; that is where we became acquainted. Loving the heat, but sadly cannot take the cold or the frost. I shiver at that thought.

My friend Dahlia is an upscale flower and is very showy, winning awards for her beauty. Very celebrated, she is in many flower shows, acquiring awards in first and second place. The points that Dahlia shows off on her petals are perfect, and they are just so magnificently shaped like royalty. Dahlia has a hollow stem, and that is why the cold gets into her body. I shudder at the thought.

Dahlia's friend, Begonia, is a rather difficult one to handle. She really is a sun worshipper, but do not show her the cold at all. So fussy. She likes to be kept close to being almost indoors, too much sun makes her wilt at the thought. Begonia is beautiful, hanging her petals and colors. Pink is the most common, but Begonia told me a story that her cousin is yellow. They hang in the shaded area of your porch or under a tree, so they do not get sunburned. People love them for their beauty, shape, and color.

Orchid loves attention to detail. She's very easygoing and grows well with little attention. We often say she has a mind of her own. But who put her on a pedestal? Orchid comes to life year-round, preferring the indoors. Often, she gets tired of standing up and needs a little help. That's where Moss comes in. Moss helps to ground the roots of Miss Orchid, allowing her to bend gently. They have long, curvy spines, creating an exotic look. Orchid has many species in her family lineage - six that I know of. She doesn't like to have her roots too deep in a pot. It seems she lives a shallow lifestyle.

My most popular friend is Petunia. We hang out all summer. She gets her name from the English and Scottish vocabulary, meaning delicate yet so strong. Petunia loves to sprawl across the ground, spreading wherever there is room for her. The saddest part is she only grows one season, leaving us with memories of her summertime beauty.

Often, she trails her curls down or sometimes up with a little help. Originally from Argentina, Petunia is a showy flower. She dons a multitude of outfits, ranging from pinks to mauve to black plum, oranges, reds, stripes and even spots. You could say she's a little showy. Petunia comes in different shapes and sizes, leading to a very versatile lifestyle. It's as if she's always ready for action. She once told me that her seeds are tiny and you only need to bury them in a little bit of soil.

Sometimes, the seeds get washed away in the rain, so we have to be very careful and water them gently. Petunias have bright green foliage, and their stems make them top-heavy. They spread like crazy and need lots of room to grow. They love to hang, so we get to enjoy their beauty. "Oh, I do like the stripes on you! I'm so envious of the different looks you can wear," I tell her.

"You can come visit me anytime. You brighten my whole planter. Besides," Petunia says, "you keep the bugs off me," and she laughs all the way home. I will love my red friend forever. What a silly name, Petunia.

Petunia will trail, and Clematis will climb up and above, overshadowing us all. Her name is of Greek origin. The neighborhood gossip starts at Clematis's house. She loves to hang and look down at you. Clematis can see forever down the path and certainly does not want to be walked or trampled on. Living her life on a trellis makes her strong in the wind. She is everyone's favorite, mostly in blue shades are her favorite looks, though I have seen her sprouting a new yellow design.

In the early spring, she shivers, showing up as the sun strengthens. She tends to face the sun. "Brr," she says, "it's cold in this ground. All my dead leaves have finally fallen off, and my new ones are sprouting." Little care is needed for my friend Clematis. Marigold is planted at her base.

"Once, I had seven petals on my body," Clematis told Marigold with delight. "I just have to be strong on my own." She sighed.

"Clematis is such a needy friend, always depending on someone to hold her up!" everyone exclaimed together. That made everyone in the garden laugh out loud. Clematis is our lookout plant, watching for who comes and goes.

Some of us flowers live a life of luxury in well-manicured gardens. Such a life of luxury, yes, they are spoiled. They came from a very upscale nursery and had guardian people tending to their every need from day one. Some of us have fewer things to keep us on the straight and narrow. They call us "Field Trash." "Oh, the carefree life," I sighed out loud. One needier plant I heard about in the nursery is the Azalea.

Azaleas like the Sun but prefer the shade. They are planted in spring and fall when it's cooler but like the light. "Really, Azalea, make up your mind!" A born leader she is!

Then there's the Miniature Rose, another needy specimen. She is a rose, alright, but a very selective one. Let me tell you, her name is of Latin descent. Her family called her Rosa or Rosanna, but everyone just shortened it to Rose. That name really does suit her; everyone will agree. She has small buds and is a petite little shrub plant. "Hmm," I say, "a Rose by any other name will not cut it."

Chapter 3
Life on the Wild Side

Not everyone comes from a nursery bed with a guardian looking after them. Some have just blown in from who knows where and make their claim to Mother Earth right where they land. I call them squatters. Down the path is such a place. Come with me. There she is, Wild Rose. I'm ashamed to admit I know her. The name "Wild" fits her for sure.

Look at her, a prickly old bush. Who can ever get close to her? Living wherever she finds a spot. Someone blew in alright, I think, straight from the wild. Spreading her wild side, now she's the "Wild Child" of the flowers. We are ashamed, but she has her own beauty. On top of this, Wild Rose is popular in North America, a native to the North American lands. They even named her Flower of a Canadian Province.

"Yes," I muse, "what a story she could tell us all." Her delicate petals are paper-thin, usually in pink or white or a combination some of us would be delighted to have.

"She is well guarded," Lilac speaks up, "with all those thorns."

"Oh, she's so bushy," says Clematis.

Look at those blooms all over amongst the thorns. She thrives in the very cold climate; some say she can survive in the Arctic. She has a cold feeling about her. She loves the sun, though. It makes her branches very hardy. Did I tell you she has a yellow center? I wonder how she could ever get close to anyone as she is so prickly and thorny. I feel she is like this for a reason. Everyone has their guard up for some reason or another.

Lupines, from another lifestyle, grow in the rockiest spots under the sun! They are from Atlantic Canada, and they are new immigrants to Western Canada. Welcome, Lupines! Lupines are tall and grow in multitudes. The bees really like them. Pink, white, yellow, and purple - wow! And you spread your seeds when the winds blow, finding a nice rocky spot protecting your growth. Lupine, you stand so majestic and tall. Standing erect like the Eifel Tower, you look so majestic.

Then there is my other friend, "Do you like my eyes"—Black Eyed Susan. Susan is very bright when she first comes out but fades fast. Growing tall and cultivated, she came from the other side of the country. She is bright and cheery looking. She has gotten the name of a commoner, said the group uneasily. She has a very dark center to her, like her mascara has run down, or she got into a fight, exclaimed everyone. She stands up for herself, that's for sure.

Black Eyed Susan and Wild Rose sure make a country-living pair. "Oh, the stories they could tell makes my petals curl," said Clematis.

Her cousin is a rusty old color flower they call Cherokee Sunset. Essential to the meadows and combined with grasses, they have long and sturdy stalks. They are called Cherokee Sunset because they have all the colors of the sunset: yellow, orange, bronze, and mahogany. Many people love to have them as cut flowers inside their homes.

They have another great friend, Sunflower. Sunflower wears a big yellow bonnet all the time. She's over six feet tall and sometimes short and stout. They are very snobby looking, always looking down at us. But they have lots of seeds to spread. They drop, blow, and grow wherever there is lots of sun. I have heard of some getting caught in the cracks of the sidewalk and growing from there, so lucky are they. The more sun they get, the happier they are. Bright yellow is the most common color with brown centers, but I have seen orange and red sunflowers. I wonder where their ancestors are from. I hear they are relatives of the Daisy family. Plus, they are forever getting their portraits painted by artists.

Sunflower has a use, after all. When they are finished growing and the bonnet has fallen off, the birds love to pick at the seeds deep inside the bonnet's face. Sunflower is the cheeriest flower of us all. The more sunshine, the taller she will grow. I would say she is outstanding in her field.

Oh, have you met Sweet William? Some call him the "catchfly".

"I rather like Sweet William," said Lilac. The girls like to tease, singing in their path, "William, you are a catch."

Sweet William comes from Europe. He has had a very popular upbringing in all the lovely gardens there. I also hear that Asia loves their Sweet William too. His season is very short-lived, blooming in the spring with a multitude of clusters of flowers. Sweet William's many admirers make him so popular.

Have you heard about the Poppies? Some are called Ornamental. They have a tough upbringing, coming from all over the world, but during the war, they grew during sad and happy times. The red Poppy is a symbol of remembrance, resilience, and peace. The most popular of all the species, Poppies have petals and blow in the wind ever so gently with grace and attitude. There are fields and fields of them growing wild, marking the graves of unknown soldiers and cemeteries. They stand so proud. They hold their heads up high. The Opium Poppy is the tallest. They bend ever so delicately in the wind.

I explain they are just ornamental. Oranges, reds, yellows, whites. But they have a dark side to their family. Opium Poppy is another type of Papaver, and you want to stay away from this guy. The seeds in the center are called 'Opium.' They produce an oil that is used in making birdseed and some everyday oils. There are good and bad in many types of flowers, just like in real people. They find a spot in you and catch you unaware.

The other wild child of the flowers is the Dandelion, many call him a weed. He plants his seeds wherever he feels like it. He is pretty bright yellow, showing off his delicate white fluffiness that we like to blow. Let's chat about the Dandelion! Some call them a nuisance, others like them. Bright yellow, toothy, and very leafy, they have deep roots that go down into the soil for up to twelve inches, sucking all the water out of the soil. Dandelions can be a nuisance in yards, but they have a lot of nutrients, such as vitamins and minerals. If anyone has high blood pressure or diabetes, they should not digest this weed-like flower. When you see the white fluff of a dead dandelion, you may want to blow it. But remember, you are spreading their seeds all over. So be careful.

Chapter 4
Toughest Friends

We all have those kinds of friends who are never there to help us when we need them the most. They survive on their own, no matter what. They never ask for help. Sometimes, they show their sunny side; at other times, they rear their ugly side.

Yes, I am talking about the Cactus, our hot-weathered friends. You might think camels are tough and can go for a long time without water, but these guys are just as resilient. Covered in sharp needles, they protect themselves from insects and birds. These insects and birds can store water in their bellies by getting in between the needles of the cacti, which is where the cacti store all their water.

Cacti can survive in the harshest of conditions, usually the dry desert, because of their water supply. They love being dry. So, if you have one as an indoor plant in your home, you don't even need to report it for 3 or 4 years. They grow so slowly and most likely will bloom in the spring, symbolizing new growth. They are slow-growing but vital to our environment.

Lady Slipper, my dear old friend, has been picked on for many years. Now, because she lives in the wild, you cannot pick her. She needs to reproduce in the natural environment so there will be an abundance of Lady Slippers for years to come. So please, if you come across dear old Lady Slipper, just greet her and leave her be; she will be okay.

Hey, have you heard of my friend, Daffodil? Always the first to the party in spring, they shout, "Let the spring begin! We are alive!"

After their long winter nap, they shed their winter skin and emerge in lemon yellow. It is a tough life, so it's no wonder they are ready to burst their skins early in the season.

What a tough life the Gladiolas, living in the ground until August. While everyone is out sun tanning and enjoying life, they are beneath the ground, keeping warm. Once we are all tired, they steal our thunder. It's said that Gladiolas pierce the heart with their petal shape, causing such infatuation. This always makes me laugh out loud.

Sweet Peas are the last hurrah at the planting season for all of us. They are planted after the last frost of the season and remain there until August before making their debut. Going out in a blaze of color, they produce the sweetest smell for such little guys. My aunt lives in an English Country Cottage where the Sweet Peas live an informal life. Sometimes they intimidate my friend, Petunia, because Sweet Peas can also trail. "Always a copycat," says Petunia. Every color comes alive where Sweet Pea is concerned. Of course, Italy and the Mediterranean coast are full of my friends.

Chapter 5
Friendship

Friends are so diverse. Each one has a special place in our hearts. They come in many shapes and sizes, but they are there for us during good and bad times. Regardless of whether it is raining or the sun is shining, in the winter or the summer, they bring us warmth. Just like our flower friends, they have feelings too.

When you think of how to describe your "best friend," you think of words like affectionate, loving, warm, and charming. Handle them with loving care. Friends bring happiness into our lives. They ease our stress, providing comfort and joy, and prevent loneliness and isolation.

No matter your friend – long, tall, thin, prickly, smelly, stinky, or even trailing in beauty – each one of them is your best friend. If you treat them with kindness, they will live and take care of your heart.

Just be yourself; you'll always be beautiful that way. A flower that feels appreciated will always do more for you than you expect. You are loved, no matter what kind of flower you are.

The End:

Thank you for embarking on this journey with Marigold and her friends. She has so many other friends, too many to name. Just remember, when you see her in the garden, think of this journey with her.

BOOK OF K

A story about Life as a Library book.

Photographs and Artwork By Sandra m Heavens

Prologue
WILL YOU REMEMBER ME?

How do I look when you open me?

What does it mean if you turn me over?

Where do you start?

At the back or maybe at the bottom?

How do I look —

Are my pictures enough?

Where are we going?

I do not know.

It has been a while.

Take me with you.

I have so much to say.

On any day or any night, I'll be here.

Please put me on your nightstand.

Let me be the last thing you touch

Before you turn off your night light. Goodnight!

Chapter 1
All About Me

When I was small, I was eager to learn. I had so much I wanted to tell the world. There is so much knowledge to share. Mom and Dad were both famous books.

Both were from the same country; "The Land of Never Too Much" and "Always Something to Read". They saw me in a bookstore on a shelf for the people who wrote literature. Mom was a Thesaurus of sorts. Her cover was red in color, and dad was the big green Encyclopedia, a short version of everything and anything. I am so proud!

Growing up was fun, but enough is enough. I need to be out sharing my life. I am a small child's version of the Book of Knowledge, named after me, of course. I have information about the word "inspect". The word means to view and examine carefully.

What about the word "phony"? It means you are a fake, not real or you are not a genuine person. It was hard to grow up expecting so much from myself. I deserved a service medal, which means a medal given to me for all my good service and spreading knowledge. All Children are valuable. I wanted to be called "K", but my dad said that is the abbreviation for a King or a Knight. Hump, I am not one of those…yet!

It was time! So, my wonderful Mom and Dad had to be told…I was going to join the library.

Chapter 2
In the beginning

They took it hard but knew I was strong enough. I was no longer a child, and it was time to turn the page. The knowledge you gain is then carried throughout your life. The adventures must be shared, so other people may learn. I left home while I still knew everything, laugh out loud!

Being small and thin, I know I will be able to fit in. I said my goodbyes and shed a few tears, leaving some water stains just for old times' sake. There was no turning back as I was on my own.

I marched up to this big building full of windows and doors. Finally, someone opened those heavy doors, and I snuck in. I jumped up and left myself sitting in the "incoming" box, waiting for my turn to be put on the shelf. This is such a big room.

It is a place of learning. There are stories in here that make you believe and some stories that scare you. I see newspapers to read, magazines to browse, books from the past, present and on into the future.

There seems to be one of everything. Sometimes, the books are written by the same person…they are famous. It is a fun place to go! Every day is a new adventure.

Looking around, there are big shelves and small shelves; everywhere, there are books, look at all the places they have been. Moms and Dads, children, babies in strollers: they are all here. They are walking around, stopping to stare at books, pulling them out and putting them back. Children sitting in little chairs, big chairs. Oh, look, there is a little grey-haired lady reading stories to a group of children. How exciting! I knew I had made the right decision about moving out and coming to the library. I thought it would be quiet and lonely, but it was not.

Surely someone would want me. It was finally my turn! The man in a suit and tie kept looking at me, turning my pages. Oh, I hope he doesn't see my leaving home tear stains on the clear white pages.

This is a huge inspection. I've never had someone flip me over, turn me upside down, and try to break my back; my spine is just fine, thanking you, sir!

I must be the right size, height, and weight. He told the other lady that I was clean as a whistle, not even tattered. I was all in order, nothing was missing. YEA: I was picked. I finally made it to the big times. I am a real live book in the library. What an honor!

The man printed a big letter out and the name where I was made and put this on my spine. "K" is the letter they gave me because my mom always called me a Book of Knowledge.

She said I knew everything! I sure miss my mom and dad. Perhaps one day, they will come to see me in my new place of honor. Being placed quite roughly onto a wooden shelf, I was between the "J" relations and the "L" family. I am so excited.

My first night alone, and I am going to keep calm and closed tight tonight, excited about tomorrow's adventure. It is a little scary all alone. Night lights are on so we all can see where we are. Everyone was busy putting books to bed and turning lights out.

"Good night," they yelled as the last light went out. Later, I was listening to some of the other books talking ever so softly in case others were trying to sleep from their busy day.

Suddenly, a young gentleman came along with a duster. He was tickling me.

I am very ticklish, and I was trying hard not to giggle out loud. He stopped and checked the sign above me, which said, "NEW ARRIVALS". He stopped his dusting, checking all of our new arrivals over. I think he heard me giggle and put me back on the shelf to sleep.

I slept long and hard, dreaming of my family at home. I knew in my heart they were ok in their own bookshelf at home. I bet they miss me. "YAWN", oh, I need to stretch.

Morning is coming through the small and big windows. You can see the little dust particles in the brilliant sunshine. Everyone is stirring.

Chapter 3
Life on a Shelf

The library is "OPEN", says the sign. All is quiet, and now here come the people.

A group of schoolchildren came first, followed by their teacher. They were running everywhere.

"SHH, you need to be quiet," said the teacher. I giggled, but Mr. J told me to stay strong. Mrs. L just glared at me. I tried not to cry. I wondered who would be the first to look at my pictures and read all about me. Here comes Kenny; he just looked at me and kept going. Mary took me out and put me down and in the shelf backwards. *Hey*, I wanted to shout. Louie came and took me and a bunch of other newbies and placed us on the table.

Last night, I learned there are books on almost everything. "ISLE" is a book on Islands.

There are thousands and thousands of small islands in the world. He is from Hawaii, where it rarely ever gets cold.
"Monty", he came from the Rocky Mountains in Canada, WOW!

"Master C" came from the Sea. There are many Seas in his book. It was hard to tell which one he really was.

"Miss L" was a laundry girl who ran washing machines and sometimes took money from people to clean their clothes.
"Little S" was a Snowman. He was all about storms.

Sometimes the Library looks like a storm hit it. There are books all over. Those librarians, they soon get us back in order. They are the mom and dad of the library.

I am "K". I am the eleventh letter of the Alphabet. There is even a book about the Alphabet. I like to think of myself as the "Key" person on the shelf. I am here to provide facts and figures that you will find interesting to read and help you grow.

My letter makes up all sorts of other words and sounds. My mom said my letter is key to the world of knowledge. OH, I am getting carried away...I am still on the table; I am waiting patiently to be taken to someone's home and read.

Stay tuned...it will be my first time out of the library.

Chapter 4
A Waiting Game

It is a long wait… I am listening to the lady tell the children how to take me home to read me. First, you need a Library card with your name on it. Then, you take the book to the counter, where a lady will date stamp your back, then another date with when I must be back on the shelf.

"OH, it's a very exciting time," I was thinking out loud when suddenly Sarah came, and then Tommy, too. They are looking at my pictures. I hope they pick me.

I want to feel that stamp on my back and go to someone's home. Mrs. Willy, the Librarian, told the children all about the Book of Knowledge and how very important I am. I'm blushing with pride. "Gee whiz," I said to myself. I am embarrassed with so much attention.

I am going home with Sherry. I am excited to see where Sherry lives. Sherry is excited, too.

Two weeks…bye everyone. Save my space on the shelf.

We take a school bus back to the Charming School. It seems like such a long ride sitting on the seat. I fell out of Sherry's backpack because she did not close it. I fell onto the floor: "Ouch, that hurts." Jerry picks me up and dusts me off, and places me on the seat next to Martha.

"Phew," I almost got stomped on.

"Hey, I can't see!"

It was a long time till I came out into the light. I was on another desk. The room was huge compared to my little space.

This will be a new experience for me.

That night, I got opened. It felt so good to see the bright light. Sherry was looking at my pictures again. "That's ok," I thought. "She's getting to know me. I have a desire to belong and not mess this visit up."

Oh dear, she closes me up. I am so sad. Goodnight, she says, and places me roughly onto the floor. I wonder if the other books are missing me.

Every day is a new adventure. Life is like a road! A journey from one place to another. "Alpha" is the beginning of the library. He always said good night first. I miss my friends.

Good night, I cry to myself.

Chapter 5
A New Day

It is morning, and I am still on the floor. Just great, I think. Another day goes by!

Sherry bends over and finally picks me up. Sherry's mom is helping her look up information from my pages. I am so excited to share. Finally, I feel like I am growing up. Sharing is so much fun, providing all my information so that others may learn.

Sherry must write a book report, and she is going to write about me. I am so happy.

The Book of Knowledge. "That's me," I want to yell out! Between my covers are different references in alphabetical order.

"Wow," said my inside voice. She is going to write all about me. How can I pass all my information onto Sherry and then onto the next person and their family... Gee, I hope there will be a next...

The word knowledge means gaining from the actual experience of something said or done and remembering all that information. There is so much inside me that I think my covers will burst with pride from all the words and pictures on my pages. Knowledge is important.

Read books, take notes with a pen or pencil, and encourage others to do the same. Sherry is writing all about knowledge and using examples from inside my pages.

She is reading about William Shakespeare, the great writer, and Christopher Columbus, the explorer, and then ballet, dancing, singing, building, and more.

Sherry hands in her book report. All about me! Sherry titled her report "You Always Have Room to Learn". I was so sentimental I felt like crying.

This was no time for tears.

Mr. Handle, her teacher, is looking at the report. In the meantime, James is asking Sherry to lend me to him. Gary wants to look at me, also. Oh, so popular!

How did Sherry do?

"Hmm," said Mr. Handle. "Sherry," he continued, "a lot of thought and work went into your report. I had not one minute that I was bored. You read a Book of Knowledge like it was a storybook. Your report is excellent." Mr. Handle was smiling from ear to ear as I sat on his desk feeling so proud; the kids were all wanting to read me next. Mr. Handle exclaimed, "You can never have too much knowledge."

"Ahhhh," I am feeling overwhelmed.

Off I go into the backpack going home. No, wait, wait…no…nooo… I am going back to the library. Shucks! I am feeling sad, although I am excited to see my friends on the shelf again. I arrive just before closing and in time to be checked for any damaged pages. Good shape, that's me. Mrs. Crook, the new librarian, takes me over to my shelf.

What a greeting I am getting from all the others on the shelf. Greetings from "A", "J", and "L". Even "R" and "S" are waving! We have so much to talk about tonight after the lights are dimmed. We all talk quietly so as not to disturb the other books. Here comes the janitor with his duster, time to say, "Good Night."

Chapter 6
Holidays

Yawn…stretch, it's morning, and I am on the shelf resting. We had a busy night, but already more children are coming down the aisle exploring and looking at us.

No, wait, they are all reading about me. I think I'm going to go on another adventure.

I sure hope it will be another great adventure. Not all are. Sometimes a book is taken from the shelf and replaced back next week, having never been opened. You can never read everything, but you need to try and read as much as you can.

Over the days, weeks and months, I have been looked at many times. I have been thumbed through and taken out, put back and on and on it goes. It has been many years since I came to the library. My pages are well-used and marked up. I heard the Librarian telling the manager (the top guy in charge), "I believe it is time to order a new Book of Knowledge". This one is worn out. Perhaps we could get a full set?" she exclaimed.

Feeling tired and sad, I knew my days at the library were ending! It has been a great experience, and I have had lots of love and some not-so-good times. My days are numbered. My old friends at the library are now gone, and new friends have taken their place. Lots of new stories to share.

The New Year is here, and I have been sitting all holiday season. No one took me home. I miss everyone and wonder how they are doing.

"Oh," here comes a big box and many books are being tossed into it. I whispered to "Isle" from the Islands that I wished I would get picked.

"Hoorah," I did get picked up and put gently into the box. One of my pages is very loose. Please fix me before you send me on.

The Librarian boxes us up. We are to be shipped out.

We sit in the storeroom in the back of the library. It is very drafty and cold and dark in here.

Where will we be going? No one comes to talk to us or tell us what is happening.

I cry myself to sleep…

Chapter 7
Heading Home

The day has finally arrived. All the boxes are being put into a big truck. We are excited.

"I'll take the heaviest box, Joe," he yells.

"Ok," stated Brian. "I'll give you directions to the 'Secondhand Store'."

After bouncing along in the truck for what seems forever, it finally stops, and the back door is opened. We are here…a real store where someone can buy us and take us home to live.

I see so many people. I am on the top shelf now, a little worn out but still a good read.

I hope to be going to a new home. It is very dark in here when they turn off the lights and lock the doors. There is no Mr. Cleaner to tickle me.

There seems to be a book sale! It's after the Christmas Holidays, and everyone is eager to get out and stock up to get ready for a long winter ahead. The sign says, "Hard Covers $1.00, Soft Covers .50 cents, comic books are" free."

Does no one read those anymore?

People are mingling, talking, picking up, and putting things back on the shelf. I am all alone.

I will take a snooze. I awake with a start. The sale is going on for several more days yet. It's storming out. I guess no one will come out today.

Suddenly, an elderly lady, a "grandma" type with grey hair and glasses, appears. She has lots of snow on her coat, takes a cart and starts to walk up and down the aisles. She puts knitting materials and a book on crocheting in her basket. Still pondering all the books, she takes many. Glancing at the pages, she puts some back while others go in her cart. Oh dear, she's finished. It is not my lucky day.

It is a quiet night but very chilly inside. We are all huddled on the shelves trying to stay warm. No one is talking. A few days go by, and the sun is shining in the windows today.

The door to the shop opens, and guess who appears: "Granny"! I just sit all by myself and wait. It is warm in here. I am wedged in somewhere between Art and Science novels. There seems to be no place for me anymore. I will shut my eyes and relax.

I find myself dreaming. When I'm floating comfortably on a cloud, I am awakened by the rustling of paper and the ringing of a cash register.

"What is happening?"

Chapter 8
Home at Last

Where am I? Why am I feeling heavy? Something is on top of me. It is dark, and it is cold. Where am I going? I try to keep warm. I'm half asleep again as we seem to be driving along a bumpy road. Thump! I awaken to a warmer place, but it is still very dark and quiet. WOW, I am being taken out of a bag! Granny! Watching carefully, Granny has a warm cup of tea and a cloth. It's my turn. She picks me up, turns me over, and dusts me off.

Not the scissors! "No," I try to yell as Granny cuts all the loose threads from my binding. After looking at all my pages, she takes out all the dog ear folds. Finally, after what seems to be forever, she is finished. I am exhausted. I am placed on a grand old bookshelf, which smells like furniture polish. I am placed next to "D", the dictionary fellow I once knew. I see "Rod" and his Rocky Road maps. "G" for Gary is here also. He likes Halloween Gravesites.

It has been days. I am still on the shelf, and weeks turn into months. I am dusted regularly and sometimes taken off the shelf and dusted behind. Granny has given me a home.
Sometimes her family takes me out, but I always go back to the same familiar place.

It seems everyone is still learning and sharing. To be a Library book has been very rewarding.

It is part of life's journey. Thank you to everyone for using a Library. Thank you for using my Knowledge in your life!

YOU DID REMEMBER ME

Acknowledgments

Many thanks to the Parkdale Writing Guild, especially Evelyn Millions, for her knowledge and guidance. Thank you to Jayne Kazi Tani for believing in me.

Photo acknowledgment, John and Ronald Heavens.

ALWAYS BE WITH YOU

A story about family life after a tragedy strikes the family.

"A Family that plays together stays together," so the saying goes…

Chapter 1
Our family

My name is Stephen, and I am 10 years old. My family includes Mable, my mom; dad, John; brother, Myles; and sister, Rosemarie. Myles is 12, and my little sister Rosemarie is just 4. We have a pet hamster named Harley, who is a white Albino hamster with red eyes. We also have two goldfish, Goldie and Flake. They are my sisters' pets, but I have the job of feeding them daily.

Harley is our newest addition to the family, and his story is unique. We all live in the house at 154 Piccadilly St. in a big city near rivers and lots of parks, bike paths, and a great "Ye Olde Ice-cream Shop". We consider ourselves very lucky people; my dad always reminds us of that.

Myles and I go to private schools called "Twin Butte". Rosemarie is in a Kindergarten class at "Over the Rainbow". We all participate in many sports. School starts at 8 o'clock in the morning, and we are home by 3 o'clock in the afternoon. Rosemarie goes every day from 10 o'clock till 2 o'clock.

Chapter 2
Getting to know us

I have a best friend, Stanley. We grew up together as babies. I have been told that Stanley and I do everything together. We ride our bikes mostly, go to the river, throw rocks, and catch frogs. Most of all, Stanley and I like the same things. He already has a hamster. Stanley was lucky; he got one way before I ever did.

It took a lot of convincing for my parents to agree that just because Stanley got one, I should too. My mom and dad told me I had to earn the respect to have a pet. So, I saved and saved all my money and my allowances and did extra chores. But Myles's friend, Marty, had a hamster that he couldn't keep any longer. Mom and Dad said I could have him.

One day, I came home from school, opened the mailbox, and found a brown paper bag in there. It moved! I screamed and jumped back, dropping the bag. I thought for sure Harley was inside, and the boy left the hamster in our mailbox. Myles heard my scream and came running, laughing at me. Here it was, just a bunch of wires in a bag. I laughed, too, at my silly behavior. Who would leave a pet in a mailbox? It so happened that Marty brought over Harley that evening: cage, food, shredded paper, and soft straw for his bedding. I had to buy some food and keep him happy. I am in seventh heaven, delighted with Harley.

Cossie was a neglected dog and was about 5 years old when he came to live with us. Sad, but it has a happy ending. Let me tell you about him.

Cossie lived with a family a few blocks away. He was tied up most of the time because his owners ran a day home for children under age 5. Cossie was always bugging the kids and taking their snacks. His little bed was in a tiny space next to the refrigerator. When the children were playing with their magnetic toys on the fridge, poor Cossie had no space. The family had a very busy lifestyle, and Cossie was left alone most of the time. Our neighbor, Mr. Smart, was telling me about this dog as he knew the family. He said if I hear of anyone looking for a nice dog, to let him know; the family had to relocate to another city, and Cossie wasn't allowed to go.

As Mr. Smart was telling me about this dog, I could see from a distance a black spaniel sitting in the driveway, looking sad. I must tell my dad. I was devastated as to what might happen to this dog. We had a family discussion at the meal table that night, and we all agreed that we would take care of Cossie by feeding, walking, and loving him lots. Cossie came to live with us. He is a loving dog and is quite the protector over Harley. His new bed is with Myles; they have become very close. A new lease on life for Cossie, happy with his new loving family.

Chapter 3
A Different Day

Today was like any other day in my life. I got up, fed all pets, ate breakfast, and headed off to meet up with Stanley. We usually meet at the end of the street where our houses join up. We ride together, sometimes taking a longer route to school or cutting through the park.

Today, we are taking the longer route along the river, skipping stones in the river, and then off to school. We could never be late, or our bikes would be taken away. It seems like a beautiful day, and my mind is planning things Stanley and I could do on the weekend. I look around my class to see that everyone is daydreaming; spring is in the air.

Finally, the bell rings. Yahoo, time to blow this place. I'm waiting for Stanley because that's what friends do. We both have enough money, so we're going for ice cream. I always get Tiger, and Stanley gets Vanilla. We ride off together.

We sit outside Ye Old Ice Cream Parlor, planning our weekend together. We decided that we would build a fort in the forest behind Stanley's house. I must look after Rosemarie too, but she likes to get dirty, so it's perfect. I will have to ride home fast and take Cossie for a walk. What a great day, and the weekend, I cannot be happier.

I awaken with a start; today, I see Rosemarie walking to catch her school bus. I am yelling, "Be careful, I'll see you soon." She gets on her bus and shows her new dolly to her friends.

"Hey, is Myles riding my bike?"

"What is happening here?"

Mom and Dad are sitting in the dining room having an adult talk. It seems like that's all they do, talk about adult stuff. I carry on following Rosemarie's bus between stops. Myles is riding alone today, which is unusual. You see, I am with them, and I can see and hear them, but they do not see or hear me.

About 6 months ago, when Stanley and I were at the park eating our ice cream cones, we got up to leave, standing at the corner. We were saying our goodbyes. Stanley went his way, and I crossed the street to go mine. As I was crossing, out of the corner of my eye, I saw a speeding car.

As I awake, I knew I wasn't with my family in real life anymore. Floating above my body, I could see everyone, but they couldn't see me. I cried, but no one could hear me. My family was crying too. A doctor was talking with them. That night, I could feel the heartbeat of my mom and dad. I felt their tears falling from their cheeks.

Myles is looking after Harley now, and Cossie is asleep on my bed. Myles is being very gentle with Harley, although he's not his favorite. Rosemarie is tightly tucked in bed with her dolly under her arm. Goodnight, sweet sister.

Chapter 4
Where Am I Going

Today, I am visiting my grandma and grandpa. They are on a cruise.

Wow! It's a very big ship in that huge ocean. They seem to be having fun meeting new friends.

Over at the Jenkins' house, they must be celebrating something.

"Yes, Sonny's birthday," I wonder.

They sure are having fun. I can't believe how old he's getting.

"Hey," said Sonny, "why is the light flickering?"

"It is me, Sonny. Stephen," but he can't see or hear me. Happy Birthday, my friend. I sure miss you.

"Look! A huge storm is brewing, I better get out of here."

There are so many people I see, and I miss them all. I want to visit each one, but today there isn't enough time.

I come by the house, Mom is braiding Rosemarie's hair, Myles is studying for a test, and Dad is painting a bike for Rosemarie. Harley is asleep in his bedding, I can hardly see him, and Cossie is with Dad because Dad has a cookie that Cossie thinks he needs.

I am laughing at Cossie. Mom and Dad are still very sad I am gone. Mom has given all my clothes to goodwill, someone will like my plaid shirt and basketball t-shirts.

Stanley comes over all the time to see Mom and Dad. They give him a big hug all the time.

My afterlife is all about traveling all over the place, helping people, and doing things that no one else can do. I have been asked to go across the ocean:

"India, lots of people, markets everywhere, men playing funny little instruments."

There are lots of beaches here, but no lifeguards. "Be safe, everyone," I whispered.

The earth is so big, and people are so beautiful. I am helping little ones play by the side of the road, keeping them safe from old rickety buses full of tourists. Sometimes I hold their hands as they try to cross the dirt streets.

Over there... "See," there is an older woman crying.

"Please don't cry," I whisper to her. It is hard watching people be sad, and you can't help them. I give her a virtual hug.

I hope she can feel she is not alone. Everyone has an angel to watch over them, and I like to think I am one of them.

Back at home, Myles is graduating. He has a girlfriend, Jeannie. I remember Jeannie; she was tall, thin, and didn't like me because I was a pain, she said.

Ha Ha, I can laugh now. What a ceremony. Myles is going to college, and I get to go with him. He hated me tagging along.

There is always a door open and more places and people to help. Let me take you there.

Chapter 5
Places to Share

"Wow," row after row of poppies.

"Oh, I remember this is the place that my grandpa told me about."

I see Doctor John McCrae wrote this story during the War: "In Flanders Fields, where poppies grow, between the crosses"...

Oh, my goodness, The Eiffel Tower, Paris. Who says you can't get to the top? Wow, they do eat cheese and bread along the river. My goodness, I have seen so much and helped so many along the way. I could write a whole book on the World.

It's been five years since I have been home. Rosemarie is all grown up. She is riding a brand new bike, I bumped into her, made her fall, and she is not happy.

"It's me, silly, I made you fall."

"Oh, my iPhone, really, Dad, what's with that? I never had one?"

Grandparents are in a Retirement Home together now; they have gotten so old.

Grandpa has a walker now, he is very unsteady. I can still sit on my grandma's knee and hold her hand. Grandma blows her nose, I'm sure she knows I am there. My picture is still on her nightstand table.

"I love you guys."

I miss you too."

Goldie and Flake are buried in the backyard under the old tree I used to climb. I am sure Harley is in a ball rolling around somewhere, I haven't run into him just yet.

Cossie has gotten very old, he sleeps a lot now. Dad has built a step for him to get into the car, he still loves the car rides. That will never change. I spend a lot of my free time petting Cossie. Mom is cooking.

"No onions, Mom," I yell.

Mom is president of the Mothers Against Drunk Drivers Association, always campaigning for a great cause. She joined after my accident. I tug at her apron; she turns quickly like she knows I am present. But I'm not there, she has a tear in her eye.

Chapter 6
Always with You

It is my last day to be at home. I am needed somewhere else. It is so nice to be here and see all my old places and friends. Most have grown up and moved away, gone to college. I visit Stanley a lot. He has my picture in his wallet. I sure miss him. I was always the faster bike rider, he won't admit it, but I was. I forgave the man who hit me, there is no sense holding a grudge. I think he is sorry, but I feel better forgiving him from my heart. It is nice to float, see everyone evcrywhere, everything. But never think I don't miss them because I do miss everything about them. There is nothing I'd rather do. I have learned that life is too short. We must do what we can when we can, we need to be kind to people and speak nice things to them. Be strong and loving. Learn to forgive your enemy. You never know when you might not get a chance to tell them all the great things. Just because no one can see you does not mean you are not with them.

'ALWAYS WITH YOU' NO MATTER WHAT!

Photo Credit: John William Kinnear, Coleman Alberta

A CHANCE AT LIFE

There is a saying what goes around comes around, or to put into Biblical terms the past weighs heavy on the present.

"The constant ringing of the cell phone—it is so annoying. Who is it this early in the morning?" Laura says to herself.

"Hello, this is she."

"Yes, of course," she says, pausing to gather her own thoughts.

"A daughter has a mind of her own—independence, they called it. Do I know where she is?" the caller asks.

"Of course, I don't know," her mind yells. "I will talk to her when she gets home. In the meantime, I will check with her friends. Thank you for calling." Laura hangs up the phone rather curtly.

"Of course, I do not know where she is. If I knew, she wouldn't be there," she says.

It is freezing out as she bends down to pull on her winter boots. The cell phone falls out of her pocket and across the floor. She regards it, continuing to tie her laces.

She brings the screen back to life and types to her husband: "Carey is not at school again."

She heads out to look for her, slinging her bag over her shoulder. She mutters to herself, "Why is it always my issue? No one ever helps me. Why should I give up my day? No one else ever does. Ugh," she carries on.

Sitting up straight in the car, she swears under her breath. "Start, you old piece of junk, start."

Carey, with her mustard-colored hair, is wearing a bright red turtleneck and a plaid mini skirt that barely covers the backside. Lord knows if she took a jacket; sure hope so. Now to cruise the streets. Looking everywhere, Laura sees the street people going through the trash cans, the kids on skateboards that just glare as she walks by, questioning their existence.

The stories that her parents told her of the people who fled from the war, leaving everything behind, taking only the clothes on their backs. Running for days, weeks, months, hiding in fields, cow pastures—did anyone ever go looking for them to see if they were safe? NO! They left behind families, friends, and possessions.

"Thank you for remembering," Laura relives.

She starts delving into his thoughts:

The life they must have had, that is how I am feeling—running and hiding. It's all a game because of me! What have I done?

Stan was my friend and now is my husband when he wants to be. Standing at a tall six-foot-four inches and nearly two hundred pounds, with curly black hair and a beard, what was not to love about him? Right from grade school, we did everything together. We hung out, played in the dirt, rode our bikes, climbed trees, and ran free until dark. As we got older, we were inseparable. Always inquisitive, we were just friends, weren't we?

65

The party we attended was just that: a get-together for friends. Going together and watching the girls drool over the boys and the boys groping the girls. We walked in the garden area down by the lake, looking in the boathouse window. There was Mary and Jim making out naked bodies. We giggled and ran away. Stopping by the shaded area of the old Cherry tree, grabbing Stan by the hand, and pulling off my knickers as fast as I could, we were kissing furiously. His hands were confident, but mine were more so. I grabbed his cock, guiding it towards me, pulling his buttocks forward, making the encounter that would seal our fate. A moment he would mention for years to come, full of pleasure at the memories. "Please don't," I said. "No, no."

How could we be so stupid? I thought no one could get pregnant. "What is the chance?" Stan implies. We drove to several druggists to get the morning-after pill. That would be the end of it, right? Yes, I will be safe. Stan and I were so careless, with no protection. What if? No way, never! Finding a druggist who sold us one, I was happy to take it.

The days turned into weeks, a few more went by. I didn't have my period, feeling nauseated and queasy, and my period was late! Being pregnant was impossible. When a pregnancy test confirmed my suspicions, I told no one. I had to take responsibility. This baby doesn't deserve this upbringing. I saw the doctor in charge. The nurse in the white uniform explained the procedure. These pills, so easy to end a life. I wasn't the only one in the room. "Follow the instructions carefully," she said as I laid back, looking at the ceiling. "There will be blood," the nurse told me. I wasn't alone; we were all so young. They said I would be able to go home at about five or six. Reading my book to keep my mind from wandering, should I or shouldn't I?

My turn had come. It was too late to change my mind. My secret and the procedure are over. The pain was like a bad cramp. Going home, I told everyone I had the flu. I lied to the nurse, telling her I had a ride home and someone would look after me. The sins of the father, those are the words from the Bible.

Remembering my life as if it were today, but I must concentrate now."

She begins her search.

The roads are terrible out here. I am going to Rutland Park, looking for Carey.

Where could she be? It is getting later and later. I have to pick up my son, Jack, from class. He would know where Carey is.

"No," was his reply. "She's always hanging out with those kids at the park. If they haven't seen her, no one has." I drove towards the house, surely Carey would turn up. No word from Stan; he could care less.

Arriving back home, there is a light in the kitchen, den, and bedrooms – of course, Carey is home. Who else puts on every light in the house like it is New York City?

"Where have you been, Carey?" Laura yells. "I have been everywhere. Not one person said they saw you, and you're missing your classes."

"Chill out," was her reply.

"You are grounded," I stated. "You will take the bus to and from school for the next three weeks or the rest of the semester. I haven't decided."

"I seriously doubt I can trust you, Carey," Laura speaks with tears running down her face.

Can anyone else relate? Is there help for these delinquent children? Carey is not a bad girl; she just doesn't like to obey the rules. There are rules to live by when you live at home.

Having tried smoking cigarettes now, but there is so much out there. Getting in with the wrong group of kids, Carey was a follower, not a leader. Remember the days she was supposed to be at sleepovers, and the girls snuck out open windows, returning to the same room before daylight. How does a mom know all this? Because a mom was being a sneak and read her diary – a terrible thing to do.

Moms knew everything, which is even more reason not to trust your daughter. Did my mom do this to me? Of course, she did. I was on a short rope. Nothing got past my mom. During the course of the evening, I mentioned to Stan about Carey, and he suggested perhaps a change of schools – maybe a private school. I laughed at him – like they will take Carey in a private school, and another school… she will still have those same friends. They all hang together; they have a bond.

We decided to monitor her and hope she will see the light of day. I cleared out her clothes closet, hoping to find what? Nothing. I was so relieved. There were cigarettes and matches, a few butts from weed, I presume. No notes, no addresses, or names of where she is hanging out.

Carey was receiving the help that she needed. A work in progress, Laura's initial thought. She recalled the numerous nights she had spent out in the cold, walking and driving the streets, searching for her. Days spent in Rutland Park, seeking anyone who might have seen or heard from her. As if any of them would break a bond and divulge information; most were oblivious to the time of day, let alone her daughter's whereabouts. Sleep was absent from Laura's vocabulary. No one would confess to knowing her. Who was the leader of this group that had snatched our "angel" from her family? The strain on the family had intensified. Life was on hold for the moment, even though they claimed she would be able to work from rehab. Someday, we will experience a stable family life.

The police were Carey's constant companions. Lounging at the boat dock, smoking weed, and possessing a few drugs. HOWEVER! This was all too overwhelming. Admitted to Juvenile court, the Judge recommended hospitalization. Stan did everything, paying the ultimate price to secure help for our daughter. The family was prohibited from any visitations or contact with her for several months, but as her rehab neared its conclusion, family visits were permitted, initially for short periods. Taking her out for a few meals during these visits, catching up on family events, hoping Carey would express missing us all. Not a single word. Silence. She looked good, her complexion rosy, hair neatly styled, appearing healthy. Promises were made about becoming a better person once she could return home. Despite Carey being kept informed about daily family conversations, the prospect of being a "family" again was heartening.

PAST:

Eddelton was a national railway town. The railroad ran right through the town and was a central hub for many other towns and cities. Everyone who settled in this town worked for or on the railroad. Along with working for the company, there came many perks: free train rides to various destinations always made for perfect getaways – to visit relations, friends, or simply to sightsee. Getting off the train at these destinations was the easy part; the hardest part was the language barrier. Interpreters were brought in to help alleviate the confusion and frustration felt by all.

Each couple had a sponsor to assist them in settling in. Albert and Monica had Rachael, who welcomed them with warm handshakes, hugs, and words of encouragement from the local community. There was a language barrier, but Rachel made them feel at home. Each family getting off the train was given a small home on behalf of the railroad. The home was furnished with essentials, and the cupboards were well-stocked to give them a good start. Albert had a job with the railroad, working on the train engines whether the train was immobile or running; it was his responsibility to maintain full running service. Monica took English lessons from the locals, becoming one of the ladies of the community. This couple had settled in nicely.

The long winter and an early spring brought promises of a hot, long summer. Albert and Monica took advantage of the free train trips that the railways had to offer – an opportunity to visit friends who had recently settled in Saskatchewan, friends from their old home village. They not only wanted to get news from the old village they came from but also to see a face from the past and catch up on news about family and relatives. They took a few days to get there and spent a week with these lovely folks, catching up.

Once they had returned to Eddleton, the best news of all came: Monica had discovered she was with child, leaving only a few months left to prepare.

PRESENT:

The day had finally come: Carey was being discharged. The whole family went to bring her home. She looked fantastic; everyone told her. While in rehabilitation, she was able to finish her schooling and complete an online graduation. So, what was next? The doctor suggested a week of rest to get reacquainted with her family and home. Carey had choices to make and needed to become independent again. Once at home, life began to take on normalcy. Jack had graduated and was now attending university in another city. Carey was getting very motivated. She started to volunteer at the Boys and Girls Clubs, helping with sports events. She also volunteered at the local library, reading to the children. She loved being with people and being out and about.

But Carey wanted more in her life; she wanted to branch out, make some income, get an apartment, and be on her own. Proving to Stan and Laura that she could be trusted and had matured enough, she was able to stay out later and meet up with friends. Sometimes, these lines of trust were broken. Were Stan and Laura just looking for something to go wrong? They had to learn to relax.

Carey brought home brochures on being a nurse's aid. It involved a six-month-long expensive course. We could not deny her an education; we needed to let her be independent. Stan got Carey enrolled in daily classes that involved a lot of homework and in-class hospital training. She studied hard and long to make this a success. The homework was a work in progress, but Carey managed to pass. The on-the-job training was happening at a local hospital. Carey was trained for bedside manners, teamwork, and household jobs more than nurse-related tasks. But she loved it. Her training period ended, and the hospital recommended that Carey could start as soon as possible. They thought she was going to be a real keeper with a lot of dedication and hard work.

PAST:

Monica currently was a proud mom of two children, who were two years apart. Carolina and Jon were very close, like a brother and sister could be. Albert now owned an older car. They had many friends who became family to them. Life was good, and they were so blessed.

Carolina and Jon grew up very quickly, as all children do, wanting their independence.

Jon was able to work on the railroad, as most of the young men his age did.

Carolina wanted to go to the big city a few hours away and become a secretary. This meant leaving Eddleton and moving to the city. Mountain City was a thriving oil and gas city, and jobs were plentiful. Monica and Albert had friends in the city who offered Carolina a room and board while she went to business college. Carolina moved her clothing and personal belongings to the city, while Jon stayed behind in Eddleton. Jon was quite happy staying behind, as he had found a young gal to marry.

PRESENT

Stan and Laura took turns driving to and from the hospital.

"Carey shows no inclination to get a driver's license or learn to drive," Stan remarked.

"There are often times when driving or picking Carey up is impossible," Laura added. "Kerry often finds other ways to get to and from her job."

"Many nights she takes a room with a coworker's home just so she can be close to work the next day," Stan said.

"Keen as she is, taking extra shifts, working overtime, it's time to give her more independence," Laura agreed.

Stan had found a small apartment close to the hospital that was for rent; Carey fell in love with it. Moving her in and furnishing it was more fun.

"We are finally able to see our children settled and happy," Stan noted.

"Carey's taste is not our taste," Laura observed. "Flags are her window coverings, and rock and roll albums line the shelves. Ashtrays line the table. 'Independence,' right?"

"Cigarette smoking is a very bad habit she took up, but it was a phase, right?" Laura questioned.

"Just do your best at your job," Stan advised Carey. "Live, Love, and Be Happy."

"Life is good," Stan continued. "So, everyone thought."

"Carey keeps in touch, and on days she does not, no one really worries as it's her life now," Laura stated.

"Make mistakes and you will face the consequences," Stan concluded.

PAST:

Carolina's new job in the oil and gas business brought many men, young and old, into her office. Being on her own now, Carolina rented a small home close to her work so she could walk to and from or take the local bus on those not-so-nice days. Carolina's personality and smile were contagious, full of life, energy, and love. It was not long after that Carolina became involved with Max. Older by a few years, oh, but handsome he was. They became inseparable. The love they shared showed.

When Max was in town on business, he stayed at a local hotel he called home. Turning the tiny crystal doorknob to the bedroom where their love was in the air. His lips found Carolina's cheeks, lingering there, and finding her mouth, she could taste the wine they had shared. The smell of the leather aftershave, they found their way to the couch. A snowstorm was a full blizzard outdoors tonight.

74

"Better stay the night," she whispered to Max. "I will keep you safe and warm."

His hand brushed her thigh, undoing her silk stockings. The power of his fingertips... Carolina was stimulated.

The next morning, the sun was shining through the snow and barren trees; it was a beautiful sight. They knew they were snowed in and made the best of the day.

"I have a gift for you, a friend's gift," says Carolina in her seductive way. The silver wrapping was everything on the package. Max peeled back the paper ever so gently. "It was my grandfather's," exclaimed Carolina.

To which Max replied, "I cannot accept this; it is far too great. I don't know what to say."

Carolina looked sadly at him. Putting the Fedora on top of Max's head, "There, it is smashing," she exclaimed.

Max took her shoulder, unbuttoning her dress. Leaving a trail of clothing on the floor, he slid off his jacket, unzipping his trousers, and falling back on the bed. Between the cool crisp cotton sheets, Max rolling on top, Max kissed Carolina with great urgency.

PRESENT

Carey has changed! No one could wrap their head around it. If she wasn't working at the hospital, she was locked up in her apartment with her two adopted cats, Felix and Milo.

Not answering her phone, I would often just drop by for a curious check. Often everything seemed normal and in order," Laura thought out loud.

"Do mothers worry about their daughters all the time?" she thought.

Carey seemed depressed; she claimed she was just tired.

"Then do not take as many shifts; take days off for yourself," Laura suggested.

"I'm okay, the hospital needs me," Carey always replied.

Stan was away on business as always when Laura got the call. Stan was ill and in the local hospital. It happened so quickly; there was no pain, they told her. He went peacefully.

What now? They had never talked about the 'what if' tragedies other than their children. Stan's body was flown home by his company. The company paid for the funeral of Laura's choice.

Jack and his lovely wife, Chantel, came home for the funeral.

Carey came and went, but that was Carey grieving in her own way. That's what Carey did, no emotion. Jack stayed longer as he was there for Laura.

Jack helped Laura clear out and sort all the bills and papers that go along with a funeral. Once everything had settled down, the house was up for sale.

There is no use rambling around by yourself in a big home.

So Laura downsized to a small townhome in the area she loved.

Carey helped with the downsizing; Jack took what he wanted, and the rest was donated to local charities.

There is always someone less fortunate than yourself.

Days of decorating went well; it helped to keep her mind occupied and pass the time.

Once the dust had settled, Laura would get herself involved in some charity work.

Right now, she was still a grieving wife, and it was taking its toll on her.

PAST

Back at home in Eddleton, Jon was planning his wedding to his new bride, Kathleen. The wedding was set for August. Carolina was going to be the bridesmaid. The village of Eddleton would be invited; they, as you know, all have become like family.

When you are part of the railway family, travel is very inexpensive to go from A to B. Carolina decided that it was time to bring Max to Eddleton to meet her family; after all, she was thrilled to show him off. He was going to be the father of her child. Jon met them at the rail station. Carolina was in her motherly attire with Max on her arm. Jon took her aside, had words with her, and sent them back on the next train to the city. It was all over. Not only was Carolina ruining Jon's wedding plans, as he stated to Carolina, but their parents would be most unhappy with her. Stay away, Jon stated, until the baby is born. Jon has postponed his wedding to happen well into October so that Carolina could still be a bridesmaid in his wedding party.

Unfortunately, Max would not marry Carolina. The decision was made as he was already married and had a family. Crying all the way home, Max broke the news to me that it would be in our best interest to put the baby up for adoption. Let a family who could not have any children take the baby into their lives and bring it up in a loving environment. Devastating as this was, the plan went into action. Max got me a great doctor and paid for all my medical supplies. I had no worries whatsoever. I am coping day to day; that is all that I did. Devastated about Max, life does go on. I moved out of my apartment into a home where they looked after unwed mothers, taking care of me until the very end. They place no judgment on my life.

The hospital visit was short and sweet. Labor went well, no complications. I never saw Max again, and neither of us had held or seen our baby. The nurses had whisked the baby girl away so quickly; there was no changing my mind.

Jon's wedding went ahead as planned. Life is normal, as far as anyone is concerned, and smiles go a long way.

PRESENT:

Several years have passed, and life went on. Carey became more elusive, taking as many hospital shifts as she could. Laura would meet her occasionally just to make sure she was doing well. There certainly didn't seem to be anything noticeable in Carey's looks.

Although smoking was still a bad habit that she could not or did not want to give up a precaution, the General Hospital had Laura as a contact should there be any emergencies.

Unbeknownst to Laura, Carey was missing many shifts at the hospital. When Laura tried numerous times to call Carey, there was never any answer.

Laura assumed that Carey was out at work and would call her back when she could. More than once, she did get a callback, so there seemed to be no need to be a worrywart. Laura did get several calls that Carey was a no-show. Laura would go to the house, Carey would just be dragging herself out of bed she overslept, did have a good night's sleep, and there definitely was nothing wrong.

Mother, you worry far too much," Laura quoted Carey's frequent response.

PAST:

Carolina went back to work in the job she came to love. She had changed her lifestyle and became quite the party girl. She often went back to Eddleton to attend different functions. Jon had a friend from the railway,

79

Martin, who was single and looking for a wife. Jon introduced Carolina to Martin, and the two seemed to hit it off. Martin was French Canadian, but the language barrier was not an issue.

It seemed Carolina was again with child, and Martin said he would marry her so she would not be disgraced by her family. He would raise the child as his own. The arranged marriage happened sooner rather than later. Carolina left the city and Martin; Carolina and baby Lewis were a happy family. The village people thought Lewis looked just like his daddy, and we will leave it at that.

PRESENT:

As the days progressed, turning into weeks and then months, life was good. Carey's life seemed in order. She never invited her mother over to her place and always had an excuse for Laura not to come over. Maybe she was unhappy with her job or her apartment. No one could quite put a finger on why Carey was so evasive in the last while.

Perhaps she had a young man in her life and wasn't ready to introduce him. Laura would surely get to the bottom of this. The hospital had called Laura to say that Carey had been missing in action for several days. She never showed up for her shifts; they tried to call her, and she never returned any of their phone calls. They were getting a little concerned.

Laura tried calling, but there was no answer. Laura got in the car and headed over to the apartment. Upon arrival, she knocked to no answer. Laura had forgotten her spare key. Looking in the windows, she could only see the cats on the table. Now, should she drive back home or get the superintendent to let her in? The latter seemed best. Getting quite concerned, she contacted the landlord, who came over with the master key. They went in together, finding Carey slumped over in a chair, arms hanging, syringes, needles, and patches all over the apartment. Nothing was clean and organized. Carey was deceased. The local authorities were advised, and an investigation started.

It turned out that in Carey's locker at work, there were old medications, nitro patches, and a good supply of used syringes. Carey was collecting the used needles as she emptied the trays, and the trash, and stealing the hazardous baskets full of needles. She was stockpiling the used items in her locker and using them on herself. There were weeks' worth of discarded pills. No wonder Carey was both happy and sad. Her life had hit rock bottom. Overdosed on medications and needles, the discarded needles were piling up. All those needles of everyone else's—what did they contain? A junkie is what my daughter became.

Burying your daughter was the hardest thing Laura has ever encountered. She knows that she is in a better place. There are no more chances at life for Carey.

PAST:

Carolina, Martin, and Lewis were a happy family. Carolina loved to travel, and they, as a family, took many trips to Mexico. They had a lovely villa to call their own, used whenever they came to the resort. Sharing with the immediate family, it was a great lifestyle. "Wouldn't Mom and Dad love to be here," was Carolina's words to Jon. So many memories, so many untold stories. Martin accepted Lewis as his own, and there were no more children in the family. Martin worked in the office of the railway. Traveling was a benefit for him; the family would all travel together until Lewis got into school, and then Carolina had to stay behind.

Martin was on one of his business trips to Montreal when Carolina got the telephone call. Martin had a major heart attack and had passed away. Devastated, the body was returned to Eddleton for a full burial. Carolina was left to make final preparations.

Friends had gathered in the house, helping Carolina get ready to go to the funeral, when a "Thud" sounded like a dresser had fallen over upstairs. Concerned friends ran up the stairs to find Carolina had collapsed. Trying to revive her, Carolina had passed away, another heart attack victim. What a tragedy. Not only were the family and friends having to bury Martin, but they were preparing to bury his wife as well. God rest their souls.

PRESENT:

So many years, so many unanswered questions. Laura is now focusing on clearing out boxes of old files, old papers, and documents of all kinds – fifty-odd years' worth of papers. Nothing but time as she started the dreaded job. She had papers of her mom and dad's. She had Stan's parents' papers. Surely, she could organize some of this on her own.

Piles for Jack to have, piles to be shredded, and piles of "What are these needed for?"

She will have Jack go through and sort with her. Days turned into weeks; the long winter helped her to purge.

Laura came across a brown envelope marked "certified," curious now as she had never seen this envelope before. A few coffees later, she called her friend Mona over to read what she had just read herself. Dropping their mouths in awe, there it is in black and white – Laura had been adopted. Her parents, Lyle and Maxine, could never have children, and Laura was adopted to fill the void in their life. No wonder she was an only child. Mother used to tell her they wanted no more; that was why Laura was an only child. No questions were ever asked as she had many relatives, cousins, and friends that filled that empty void.

Upon reading further in the papers, Laura finds that her biological mother was Carolina, and her father was Maximilian. No one had ever told her, even talked about her past. Now there are so many questions that need answers – how do I deal with this? Another drama, Laura says to her friend Mona. They talked for several hours, and Laura puts the papers back in the envelope. "I cannot deal with this, another time perhaps," she says aloud.

PAST and PRESENT:

Lewis has grown up into a fine young man. Uncle Jon has helped him through difficult years, and now he is on his own. Set for life, although there is no mom and dad to share it with. A job with the railroad, just like everyone else in the Village.

Laura has hired a private investigator and a lawyer to dig into her past. See what goodies they can come up with. Papers were issued, and certified adoption documents were located. It is going to be mind-consuming and take-your-breath-away moments. Information stated that Carolina

Marie was 21 years old at the time of Laura's birth, and Maximilian George was 26 years old. Neither could raise the child, so they decided to put the baby girl up for adoption. The hometowns of both were given, but both were deceased.

Several months later, much to Laura's curiosity, she had gone to the cemetery in the Village of Eddleton, wandering from grave to grave looking for her parents. Looking for answers, but will she ever know? She wasn't too sure what the spelling was or if they were even there when an older gentleman came along asking her if he could help her find someone. Showing him the names of the people, he stated there was a whole family by that last name buried in Section D. Thanking him for his help, she continued to take pictures of the graves, but nothing was there that said, Carolina or Maximilian. Not even knowing if her mom had remarried or used her maiden name. Taking a chance, Laura went to Section D. Although she was quite sure Max was buried in another town or city, she would deal with that maybe at a later date. Right, she was on a mission to find her mom. The graves she just saw were likely grandparents or great-grandparents. Satisfied, she started to leave when a young man came into sight. He walked with a purpose to his steps. Laura found a bench and waited for him to leave. She was curious about who he was going to visit. Several minutes later, the young man left, and Laura found herself being called to the grave site he was just at. Not knowing what she was there for, she found it! Her mom's grave. Carolina had the same dates as the lawyer had given her, the same names that were confirmed in writing. Taking several pictures, Laura found the cemetery chapel, going inside, saying a few prayers, asking questions that she knew she would get no answers to, but she felt compelled to ask. Whoever was listening, she asked, why? Who am I? Who was my mother? Where was my father? Do I have any siblings? So many questions, no answer. So many years had passed, and everyone took the stories to their graves with them, leaving unanswered questions. She found herself, but most of all, she thanked everyone that she was here. Leaving the chapel and cemetery, she drove around Eddleton, looking at the homes, always wondering where she lived. No one else would know about her life. She had the documentation she needed. She knew where to come to visit and talk to the mom she never got to know.

Laura had Jack and his children and their mother to call her own. There would be no more secrets. Now she was wishing her life was different but very grateful for having the chance at life.

LOST AND ALONE

Today, Saturday, is my day off from the dreaded dress store alterations. I long to make a new pink gingham frock with lace edges and puffy sleeves, something sexy, bright, and oh-so feminine. But who am I fooling? I have nowhere to wear it and no one who wants to take me dancing. I will just sit back, read a long story, and dream.

Feeling lost and forlorn, I struggle through a few lines in the book. Afterwards, I took myself to the bathroom, applying some makeup - mascara oh so thick - and a little squirt of perfume. Now, what to wear? I find a bright turquoise swing skirt and a sweater with a peter pan collar. I dress up and grab my heels and purse. Catching the local bus called the Rounder, I am off to see what is in the shops.

The bus finally arrives, and it is standing room only. All the men and women who have Saturday off are out and about. Looking around the bus, I see so many familiar faces. There are no names to put on them; I just recognize them from coming into the shop. I try not to stare at the handsome men with their wives who are giving them the evil eye. "Why are all the handsome ones taken?" I think to myself.

My stop arrives, and I am off on First Street, the main shopping area of Clyde. Window shopping is so much fun: browsing and examining all the lovely pieces of fashion. "You don't always have to buy," I think to myself. Dreaming of the possibilities is great enough.

"Well, look at you, Marie," says Millie.

"What brings you out on this lovely Saturday?" I am star-struck. Millie has a handsome man on her arm, and I am feeling a little embarrassed.

Not my best response, but I manage a, "Well, hello, Millie. Seems like you are out, too, on this spring-like day. Beats house cleaning."

The cars and trucks are coming and going down the street. Birds are singing in the trees. Dust is blowing as they haven't cleaned the streets from the long winter. After a short while of window shopping, I go into the local soda shop and order a float. There, in the back booth, is the manager I work for at the alteration place. Do I stay or go?

I have never really had a long talk with him; he is just my boss. He sees me glaring, and it is so obvious, isn't it? He calls me over, asking me to join him.

I straighten my hair and apply a little lipstick to my pouting lips. I get my float and join Matt in the booth.

"Thank you for inviting me to sit; it really is a busy day. It's the first nice day we've had in a long time." Matt is single and a few years older than me. I have just turned eighteen, and I am thinking he is about twenty-one.

Matt is very vocal at work. I suppose when you are the boss, you are allowed to be. He has reprimanded me on many occasions as my dressmaking skills are slow and precise. He always maintains that it's the quantity that counts. I like to have quality work, and that's where we butt heads.

"What brings you to the city, Matt?" he asks. I am a little shy, but idle talk always helps. Besides, he is my boss. I tell him I just feel like getting out and seeing what the shops have to offer for the season. He agrees with me, and we spend time talking about fashion and what is new on the cutting table at the store.

I drink my float, and we both get up to leave. Almost knocking him over, I desperately apologize. I feel like a total klutz. We both laugh and walk out together. Seeing as how I have nowhere to go, we walk together for a few blocks, talking fashion mainly. Seeing my Rounder bus coming, I say goodbye and get on.

The journey home is pleasant. I feel good that I had a chance to get to know Matt a little better. Having him to myself was even nicer. Feeling slightly attracted to my boss - what a terrible thought. But I am only human.

Getting home, I change into casual clothes and spend the rest of the day off cleaning, reading, and daydreaming about Matt. The alarm goes off at seven as I need to be at work for nine. I have a few blocks to go, so I ride my bicycle on this warm day. Not having to dress up for my job as I work in the back room, I take a little extra time putting on makeup, hoping to impress Matt.

Getting to the shop on time, I punch my time card and go back to the sewing machine that has been assigned to me. My table is full of clothes that need attention. I am lost at work when Matt arrives to see how the button sewing is coming along.

He asks me to come to the front of the store to see a client who is trying on a new design he has made for her. I blush. The other ladies are watching to see where I am going and if I will come back. Once at the front of the store, Mrs. Poshly is modeling a design for her daughter's wedding. Matt has designed the dress himself from the finest silks he has brought in from India.

I tell her how lovely she looks and suggest a few minor adjustments that I will make to show off her figure in the new design. I suggest a few sequins be sewn onto the top, making it the focal point of the dress. Matt seems to be okay with my suggestion and tells me I can go back to what I was doing.

All eyes are on me when I return. I have the biggest smile on my face, leaving them guessing. I continue with button sewing on the garments on the table. When lunchtime comes around, I take my bag to the lunchroom, filling the girls in. They are in awe that I have been asked.

Back at one o'clock, I continue with hemming the dresses I had started, as they have a deadline.

Matt Marsh Dressmaking and Design is where I work. I applied right away when I finished school, leveraging my sewing skills to my advantage. When I applied, he did not want to hire me straight away because I had no experience. I begged him to give me a chance for a few weeks. If he didn't like my work, he could let me go.

Mr. Marsh purchases the best fabric and has a team of cutters for each design he sketches out. I do the finishing and am never tasked with cutting. I'd love to progress from finishing, but I'm too embarrassed to ask for a promotion. I have been working here for a couple of years now, always keeping my nose to the grindstone.

Often lost in thought, the rest of my days pass uneventfully. As the week progresses, I find the Mrs. Poshly dress on my table with a note, saying, "Your dress, please apply sequins where you think the client will appreciate them." I blush, dropping the dress, I'm working on, I immediately start the task. Having it ready for her next fitting, it receives everyone's approval. Matt admires my sequin design work.

There seems to never be a dull moment in the shop. A few unfamiliar men come and go; buyers bring in bolts of material for Matt to consider. Mail arrives daily, and I often observe Matt opening it and discarding it. Not contemplating too much about that, I think if it was of importance, they would not end up in the waste basket.

Occasionally, Mr. Murray takes charge of the shop operations while Matt is absent. I don't particularly care for him. He has shifty eyes and constantly looks for things in the drawers, even looking through the wastebasket at times. Not trusting him, I keep my thoughts to myself. Mr. Murray and Matt travel together to buy materials from Paris and other European cities. I'm uncertain about Mr. Murray's role in the operations. All I know is that I don't like him.

One day I witnessed Mr. Murray helping himself to a bundle of money from the cashed register without leaving a note of replenishment, but what do I know?

On this day, I notice Matt observing me as I work. I feel self-conscious and try to speed up a little. At the end of the day, I am asked if I would like to join him for dinner. I accept. I meet him at Bennett's, a family restaurant, at seven o'clock. Once inside, I see him already seated at the table, but OH! Mr. Murray is there, too, at a table set for three. Is it really happening, a threesome? I feel uneasy but proceed anyways.

A glass of wine is being poured, and small talk circulates. I discovered that Mr. Murray has an invested interest in the Design shop. Mr. Murray and Matt haven't known each other for long, and I find this strange for two people to be in business when they barely know each other. I pay attention to the conversation between them; sometimes, they are so secretive it's hard to decipher their words. A lovely roast beef meal, Yorkshire pudding, potatoes, and carrots are served. I'm extremely nervous and eat slowly. The men take out cigarettes from their shirt pockets and engage in conversation. I feel like an outsider, not part of the scene, asking myself, "Why am I even here?" After what feels like a long evening, I excuse myself to go to the ladies' room and powder my nose. Coming back, I see them standing, waiting for me. It's time to leave. I thank them both for a wonderful meal and begin my walk home. They don't offer to drive me, but I feel safe in Clyde.

The next day at work, I'm completely ignored, as if I don't belong there. What was the purpose of the previous evening? Several weeks pass, and Matt corners me in the back room, suggesting that I move into the upstairs apartment above the Design shop. He has recently bought it and thinks it will suit my lifestyle perfectly. After hours of pondering, I accept the offer. I won't have to pay any rent as the company covers that. It's part of the perks. I wonder what kind of deal I'm getting myself into.

I don't have much furniture to bring with me, but a couple of men from the dress alterations workshop offered to move my belongings to the new apartment. The walls have been freshly wallpapered with the finest coverings. Not particularly to my taste, but I don't feel it's my place to change.

Little do I know that Matt has a spare key and comes and goes at his leisure in and out of my apartment. He never bothers me, but I feel uncomfortable with this arrangement. He insists that I make him meals occasionally, and he often brings Mr. Murray along, totally ignoring me. Sometimes he gives me money and tells me the meals to prepare for him and Mr. Murray.

One Saturday, while I am out shopping and carrying the heavy bags of groceries home, I stumble and fall. Groceries go everywhere. Feeling embarrassed, I look around, hoping that no one has seen this accident, and wondering how I will pick up all the fruits and vegetables that have escaped from my bag. A kind man sees me and offers his assistance to help me home. He carries my groceries to the apartment.

Upon arrival, I take the bag of groceries from the stranger. I insist on making him a cup of tea for his efforts. While I am making the tea, Matt walks in and gives me an evil look. I tell him how kind this man is and that I have fallen. Not seeming to care either way, I make him a cup of tea as well. Soon, the stranger leaves, and I don't even know his name after all that has taken place. Matt doesn't ask me any questions or inquire about my fall. Instead, he just tells me to make his meal and pretends I'm not there. What have I gotten myself into?

On the weekend, I invite my Mom and Aunt Teresa over for a meal. Matt is invited too, and we all sit around having a good time. Matt treats the family like his own, and I am pleased to see that. My Mom thinks I have gained a lovely young promising man in my life. Matt is the first one to leave, and the rest follow. The rest of the weekend, I neither see nor hear from anyone. It is the strangest relationship I ever think possible.

Back at the shop, I often get asked to model dresses for male clients who are buying for their wives. I feel good in the fabrics but don't appreciate all the attention the men give me. But it is for the sales in the dressmaking department. I so want to make Matt's designs a hit. Reputation and word of mouth go a long way, especially in Clyde.

Matt and Mr. Murray are going to Paris. A trip that is a spur of the moment. Matt asks if I would be interested in coming to the most romantic city in the world. He designed a dress especially for me to wear while I was in Paris. I am preparing for my trip. Having never traveled far before, I don't know what to expect. We catch a flight from Chicago direct to Paris, flying in first class. I feel like a queen. We laugh and talk like we are all from the same family. Mr. Murray still seems sly, and I am untrusting of him. Once we land, I am in awe of the skyline.

Taken by cab, we arrive at a small hotel in the 3rd Arrondissement, where the architecture is out of this world. This seems to be the part of the city where everything is happening. The locals favor this part of the city for its great restaurants. We have separate rooms, and I unpack for my three-day stay, hanging my new dress ever so carefully. I am told dinner will be downstairs at precisely eight PM, and I am instructed on what to wear, including the shoes. I find this odd, but I don't complain, as Matt is paying the bills.

After a lovely evening, Matt and I take a stroll along the River Seine. To my surprise, we are not alone. He holds my hand, and we laugh like two old people in love. I know I have been falling in love with him for many months. The feeling is mutual and odd. Watching the fireworks from a riverboat, we kiss, and the night is just magical.

The next morning, after a lengthy meeting at the fabric distributors, Matt tells me to wear the new dress he has designed for me to tonight's dinner. He says he has a surprise for me. I am nervous and anxious at the same time. Is he presenting me with another new dress he designed, or maybe making me one from some lovely fabric he purchased today? Or perhaps giving me a chance at the cutting table in the factory? Things are moving along so smoothly.

94

We are at a fancier place for dinner at a new restaurant. Tonight, there is another new gentleman at the table, a Mr. Doorman. He joins the three of us for a meal. I don't know what all these men have in common. Matt acts like he has known him forever. But I soon realize it isn't so. I am totally alone again amongst strangers.

During the meal, Matt announces that he has an announcement to make. Getting everyone's attention in the restaurant, Matt takes my hand and, to my surprise, says that he would like to marry me tonight, right here, right now. Trying not to look shocked, I am so embarrassed. Nothing like this was ever discussed, although I have dreamt of it. Am I dreaming, or is it for real? I can't believe my ears.

I plead with Matt that I would rather have a wedding back in Clyde with my Mom and Aunt Teresa attending. I have no plans to elope. Matt says it would be a surprise for my Mom and Aunt Teresa and that they wouldn't turn against me. What would my family think? I have never had sex before, and I'm not pregnant, although I am sure that my Mom would think so. Mr. Doorman has a ring, and the papers are all in order. We are married at the table. This was all planned, and I am furious. How could Matt arrange this with a man he claims he has just met tonight?

A bottle of the restaurant's best wine is brought to the table in preparation for the celebration. I drink too much because I'm so nervous. That night, Matt spent the night in my room. It is terrific lovemaking like I have never felt before. Being a virgin, Matt knows what is expected of me. I feel scared and sick at the same time.

In the morning, there are numerous other fabric-buying meetings to attend. Of course, Mr. Murray comes along like a little chaperone. Matt and Mr. Murray still leave me out of the conversations, but at this point, I'm so used to it that I don't mention anything. I'm still in wonder where Mr. Murray comes into the picture. Money doesn't seem to be an object, and they are high tippers. I don't question it, as I have never traveled to other cities before.

Another lovely meal with Mr. Doorman that night after all the buying for the next season is completed. The brocades and embroidered, heavy-looking fabric will all be the rage. They are all being shipped by boat to America.

Once back at Clyde, I return to the apartment, and Matt goes to the shop. I'm worried sick about how I'm going to tell my Mom and Aunt Teresa that I'm married. Matt and Mr. Murray come to the apartment with some furniture, placing it where they want. I have no say in the matter. There are chairs and tables and extra bedroom furniture for the spare room. Matt tells me to go to bed because I'm expected to be back in the shop by nine AM. I'm so confused, I need to talk to him about telling my Mom. I sleep restlessly, and when I wake in the morning, I see that Matt hasn't come home that night. What is going on? Where does he spend the night? Does he have a mistress?

Gathering my lunch and keys, I walk down the stairs to the shop. Should I tell the others that Matt and I are married, or should I let him tell them? I really am in a quandary. I go back to my assigned machine like always and carry on with business. At lunchtime, Matt tells me that from now on, I can eat my meals in the upstairs apartment. There is no need to bring lunch. After a hard day, I go home and make a lovely supper of fish from the market and greens. Matt joins me. Not a word about our marriage, not a word about the furniture. I finally decide enough is enough and ask him to come with me to tell my Mom. We decide to go the following day and take a bottle of wine with us.

Matt picks up the best bottle he can find, and we arrive at the house. Aunt Teresa and my Mom's friends are there too. We walk into the house, accepting hugs and kisses from all. "Tell us all about Paris. What did you buy? Is it as lovely as the pictures show?" Everyone is talking to us at once. We sit for a meal, and it is during the meal that Matt announces that he has married me in Paris. Everyone is over the moon. My Mom seems not surprised but more disappointed than anything. She isn't angry or doesn't seem to be. More wine is brought out, and we celebrate. During the course of the evening, Matt announces that we are moving the shop to an older district in Clyde, one more suitable for his business. I ask where we will live, he insists he will find us a home of our own. Another adventure, another secret, with more promises of happier times to come.

Several weeks go by. Matt has moved the shop to a much older building in the heart of Clyde's factory district. He purchased a flat, or apartment as I call it, many miles from the shop. I obviously have no input in the home whatsoever. It is so far away from the shop; I would have to take a cab to and from work, an added expense, I tell Matt. He surprises me with another announcement. I will be working from home from now on. Movers will come to the flat in the next day or two with my sewing machine and all the needles and accessories that I will need for alterations. Every day someone will make a delivery to the flat with alterations for me to do and pick them up when they are ready. The apartment is bigger and has lots more room, but why can't I go to the shop?

Matt seems very jealous of me, often asking whom I have entertained in the apartment that day and what stranger did I make tea for. I am already feeling isolated in this new place. I have no friends and wouldn't be able to get out as often. I feel I am being confined in my own place. When I

97

disagree with Matt, he comes and kisses me and pats my hair, telling me everything will be alright, then sits in silence while I serve supper. Often, he would go back to the shop and come home very late or not at all.

Below the flat, there are many coffee shops. I can see people coming and going. I sometimes see Mr. Murray sitting there with his morning newspaper. Am I being spied on? My Mom and Aunt Teresa come over for visits quite often.

One day while watching out the window, I see the mystery man who has been so kind to me when I fell. I rush down the stairs to get his name and thank him once again. He is so gentle and kind. I am so lonely for someone to talk to, and Frank, as I find out his name is, is so pleased to see me.

A few days later, there are painters present at the apartment building. They are busy painting it in a white hue with a French name inscribed on the exterior. Matt insists he is doing all this for me. He has chosen to call the apartment Chez Marie, a name inspired by mine.

Things are progressing smoothly at the apartment for work. Matt is on the go, coming and going as his work requires. I miss the company of other employees, though. An irksome issue is seeing Mr. Murray and sometimes Matt at the coffee shop, and yet no one has ever invited me there. I question myself, "What if I just show up?" But no, I can't just do that. A few months later, I discover that I am expecting a child. I share the news with Matt, revealing my pregnancy. His reaction is less enthusiastic than expected, which is a disappointment.

My Mom and Aunt Teresa, on the other hand, are overjoyed. They go ahead and buy a crib and layettes for the baby, who is due to arrive in November. Questions buzz in my mind about how I will manage to juggle between the baby and my sewing responsibilities. Maybe Matt will suggest that I should primarily be a mother.

However, Aunt Teresa's decision to move across the states is met with sadness. She expresses her feelings, thinking that she will never make her mark in Clyde. This leaves Mom and me with feelings of disappointment. Aunt Teresa and I have a major disagreement over this. I accuse her of acting selfishly. In return, she retorts that I have made my bed, and now I must lie in it. She goes on to predict that I will never achieve my aspirations of becoming a fashion lady. This harsh statement causes me to cry myself to sleep that night. Matt doesn't offer any words of comfort.

As my pregnancy progresses, I find it more difficult to move around. Groceries start being delivered to our apartment. My hope is that the baby will arrive while Aunt Teresa is still in the city. My labor starts unexpectedly one night, leaving no time to reach the hospital. Matt quickly rings up my Mom and her friend Sadie, urging them to come over as soon as possible. During the delivery, he leaves the house.

We name our baby boy Luca. We have decided on the name quite some time ago. He is beautiful, but the delivery leaves me extremely exhausted, and I need rest. When Matt returns, he is delighted to see his son, or "the boy", as he refers to Luca. What I find odd is that he doesn't hold or cuddle him.

Aunt Teresa pays us one last visit. She brings a toy chicken for baby Luca, which makes a clucking sound. He is instantly fascinated by the sound. This toy will turn into his favorite in the years to come.

While at home, I continue with my sewing alterations. A baby pram, a gift from Mom's friends, proves to be very helpful. I take Luca out for fresh air as much as I can. I even make time to stop at the café across the street to treat myself to a coffee. But I always rush home, ensuring that the evening meals are prepared in time.

Having guests over is often exhausting. Matt informs me that Mr. Doorman is in town and will be coming over. I am tasked with preparing a meal consisting of various fish from a list provided by Matt. Early the next morning, with Luca and my shopping list, I set out to buy the things I need. As I struggle to handle the bag of groceries and push Luca into the pram, a young gentleman appears from nowhere, offering his help. I thank him and offer a few coins, but he politely declines.

Back at home, I put Luca down to play on the floor and resume my alterations. After preparing a sumptuous meal, I set about serving Mr. Doorman and Matt. After ensuring Luca is in bed, as Matt doesn't want him around, I serve the meal. Overwhelmed with exhaustion, I excuse myself after cleaning up and go to bed.

The next morning, I am met with a reprimand from Matt. He criticizes me for going to bed while a guest is still at our home. He suggests that I should manage my time more efficiently when he is at work rather than socializing with the neighbors. When I try to explain that I wasn't inviting anyone over except my Mom and her friend Sadie, he doesn't listen. Instead, he raises his voice, upsetting Luca. I am certain that Mr. Murray is spying on me and making up stories to tell Matt. How else would he know about my activities?

Luca is almost two years old when I discover that I am pregnant again. Matt is insistent that he is not the father. He argues, "With all the men coming and going from the apartment and your coffee trips, it could be any one of them!" I am devastated that he would even entertain the thought.

My Mom is appalled at the thought of Matt and tells me I should have never agreed to marry such a man. "He is controlling, abusive mentally to you, and it's not good for Luca to be around him," she says. I am left wondering, what am I to do?

I am still doing alterations for the shop when one day, I take Luca on a stroll to the shop. Matt isn't there, and Mr. Murray is out. The ladies are so loving, giving Luca all their attention.

I am in the office and find that there is no money in the drawer despite bills piling up. The wastebasket is overflowing with letters and overdue bills. I am getting concerned about where all the money is going. I never have any money; it is all in the hands of Matt. He usually gives me just enough to buy the few things I need when I am sent out for groceries.

Luca is a growing boy and loves his chicken from Aunt Teresa. He seldom bothers me when I am working on garments. There comes a knock on the door one day. When I answer, it is a stranger asking a lot of questions about my apartment and the Dress and Design shop.

When I tell him he should really speak with my husband, he claims Matt is never around. I tell him what he wants to know. However, when I tell Matt about it, he is furious that I am giving strange men information. He insists I am making it up to cover my tracks for having men in the apartment when he is at work. I can't understand this as I never go anywhere anymore, and I only talk to people when I am out. I don't even go to the shop any longer as it is just too far to go.

Matt spends nights away and claims he is asleep in the office when he isn't at home. I know in my heart that there is no couch in the office, so my mind starts to imagine the worst.

Mr. Doorman is always here, it seems. Matt states he has moved from Paris to be in Clyde, where Matt's thriving business is. Mr. Murray is still seen at the coffee shops daily, pretending to read newspapers.

I am getting more and more frustrated living this life. Here I am, only twenty-two years old, with no friends and an uncaring husband. He thinks that by buying me gifts and apartments, he is loving me.

I have considered a divorce, but with a new baby on the way, I couldn't possibly manage. And besides, it is almost impossible here in Clyde. No one gets a divorce.

I am but weeks away from delivering a new baby, feeling much better with the second child than I ever did with the first. Matt is not home when baby number two comes. I call my mom, and she arrived with the midwife. Luca is well cared for with my mom, and the Midwife helps deliver another healthy baby boy. Matt will be beside himself. Two boys to continue the Marsh name.

It is the next morning that Matt arrives home. Bringing me flowers was a pleasant surprise. Mom is still at the house when Matt arrived, already knowing it is a boy that had been born. He claims he ran into the Midwife's friend who told him about the boy, as he called him. It takes us five days to produce a name: Marco. Marco is a quiet baby, not like Luca was. Marco sleeps, and I continue sewing, although I get nowhere fast as two children keep me busy.

There's so much new at the dress shop, and the bills are piling up. People are calling, and the taxman is always at our door. I wonder where the money is always going. Mr. Doorman is not in the picture anymore; I am delighted that he is gone. Matt tells me he has gone back to Europe to live the rest of his life.

I continue my dress alterations in the house. It's more convenient this way with two children. Marco is a good, quiet child. Luca is always content playing with his chicken Aunt Teresa had given him. Matt decides he would like to take the children for the day. I feel a sigh of relief and am not concerned at all. I prepare for their outing. They'll only be gone the day, but I have several changes of clothes, as children are messy. The day comes, and Matt is going to take them somewhere. He tells me he doesn't know where but will only be gone the day.

A day to myself, long-awaited, I'm looking forward to it. What will I do? I'll visit the girls in the shop and take a picnic lunch to them. I am over the moon. The day comes, and Matt, Luca, and Marco are off on an adventure. I've packed all the things necessary for the day's outing. Can this really be happening? I take a long hot bubble bath; the time is my own. I go to the shop and visit my coworkers. There's no Mr. Murray in the office, and even if there was, I'm not afraid of him. I've taken an array of fresh greens and buns to

103

share with the workers on the alteration floor. We have a lovely time, knowing there's no one cracking the whip. The day is bright and beautiful. I pack up, leave the girls, and head back to my home. I feel a bit uneasy and lonely when I walk into the room. I see little Luca, his chicken right where he left it. I spend the rest of the day visiting my mom and her friends. When I come home just after the dinner hour, I'm startled by the fact that Matt isn't home and hasn't been. They must be having a lovely day, but the children must be getting fussy by now.

Mr. Murray has arranged for a car to take Matt to the Shipyard, where Matt meets a man, a stranger. They've said little to each other, but papers and money have been exchanged. The man with the bright blue fedora soon shakes Matt's hand and quickly leaves the docks. Matt picks up the children, the valise, and starts to embark, trying not to look nervous. He has Luca by the hand and tells him a story of going on a big boat and how it's going to be an adventure.

Luca just keeps asking for his mommy. Trying to ignore the childish pleas of wanting his chicken, Luca is hushed by his father. The captain and security examine the passports, scrutinizing Mr. Brightman a bit longer, asking if his spouse will be traveling with him.

Matt declines, stating, "My wife has passed away. I can't care for the children on my own, so I'm taking them to my wife's sister in Southampton to be raised. These are my children, Liam and Mark."

The security and crew offer their sincere apologies and hope he enjoys his trip. The cabin crew escorts Matt to his room, which will be the family's home for the next ten days. There's not much room for the children to play. Matt finds that out soon enough. He's exhausted and wants to sleep, but the children are anxious and want to play. Matt didn't know the boys usually had afternoon naps, nor did he seem to care. He's glad he's escaped according to plan. Once in England, he plans to start a new life, find someone for the boys, and carry on in a new country.

The ship set sail on time, and with the police not knocking on his door, Matt sighed with relief. He had to play the part of a grieving husband. Once the ship was out to sea, Matt took the boys out on the deck. Amid the frigid air he was unprepared for, he soon realized he needed warmer clothing for the children. He'd have to keep them inside more. While meeting several couples who admired the boys, Matt tried to keep to himself. He found life boring and wanted to be on his own. Having put the children to bed, Matt went to the main dining deck. He settled in for a nice dinner, avoiding eyes when he could.

"So, it is Mr. Brightman?" asked the lovely blonde lady. "Will Mrs. Brightman be joining us tonight?" she continued. Matt replied that Mrs. Brightman had recently passed away and she wouldn't be with them on the trip. Lady Trimm gave her sincere apologies and the meal was served. After dinner, Matt went to the casino to try his luck at cards. Well after one in the morning, Matt called it a night. Fortunately, he won a few hundred dollars at poker; with this group, he didn't need to talk, which suited him perfectly. Matt stumbled back to his room, only to find the boys were awake and crying, Luca wanting his chicken, and Marco just crying because. Matt went out and found a crew member who provided him with supplies he quickly realized he needed, and some sandwiches for the boys, hoping that would give him some peace and quiet. How Marie put up with all this ruckus from the boys was beyond him. After a frantic, unsettling night, Matt was finally able to sleep. He felt as though he had just gone to bed when the children wanted up. Nothing would make them happy. He called the cabin crew once again, requesting hot milk and cereal be brought to the room, hoping this would quiet them so he could get more sleep.

After several days of unsettled family time, Matt decided to take the boys out onto the upper deck, thinking a change might be good for them. He didn't have enough clothes and realized he'd need to do laundry. As he walked about, he caught the stares and whispers of people. "There's that poor man, all alone with his two boys. You know his wife has passed away. How dreadful! He doesn't look like he has a lot of money; he's wearing the same trousers he came aboard with. Dreadful!" exclaimed the ladies passing by. Matt was displeased to hear the ramblings about him, but there was little he could do. There was so much he hadn't considered.

Meanwhile, back at home in Evanston, Marie was distraught. She called everyone she could think of and retraced her steps from the past few days, thinking she must've missed something. After visiting the alterations shop, she learned no one had seen or heard from Matt for several days. The police wouldn't immediately start looking for Mr. Marsh, as there didn't seem to be any signs of domestic violence. Marie tried to locate Mr. Doorman, but he seemed to have disappeared; no one knew of him. Mr. Murray had also vanished. "What's going on? I want my boys back!" cried Marie. After looking through all the bills and letters she could find, there was nothing to indicate where Matt had gone. Marie stayed home, fearful the children would return and she wouldn't be there. Her mom was also outraged, referring to the situation as a kidnapping. Eventually, the police filed a missing persons report for the boys and Matt. The detective on the case contacted all the fabric suppliers in Europe, but none had seen or heard from

Matt. The bank accounts were emptied, which wasn't unusual since Matt seldom used a bank. Bills and letters still arrived, threatening to sever ties with the shop over overdue payments. Marie was determined to keep the shop running, holding onto the faint hope that Matt would return safely with the children and life would resume as usual. The idea of kidnapping had never crossed her mind. Why would he? She pondered the possible motives but was left with unanswered questions.

Time marched on, and it hadn't been the best of sea crossings. Matt hadn't considered how much two children would tie him down. Looking back, he realized Marie had been an angel, managing both the house and work without complaint. Whenever Matt had a moment without the children, he used it to wine and dine, enjoying the casino aboard the ship. The seas were tumultuous, causing general discomfort for everyone. Due to the unruly seas, everyone was ordered to stay in their rooms. However, Matt was taking advantage of the circulating gossip about him. Should anyone be looking for him, they wouldn't suspect him on the ship. After all, he was a grieving widower, and the boys were visibly upset, frequently crying for their mother. Their grief would serve as the perfect cover. Once in Southampton, an anonymous associate was set to meet him and take the children to their new home.

The stormy conditions persisted, making it impossible to spend time on the decks. Passengers were confined to their rooms, and even the cabin crew struggled to deliver meals. Many became ill, emphasizing the importance of cleanliness on board. On the evening of the seventh day, a fire broke out in the engine room. Initially dismissed as a minor incident, the choppy waters made it challenging to control the fire. Alarms blared, directing everyone to don life jackets and head to their designated muster points. Handling two children made things difficult for Matt, especially since they weren't dressed adequately for the emergency. Noticing his struggle, Lady Trimm and her husband offered to take the boys with them on the first lifeboat, allowing Matt some respite. Gratefully handing the children over to the Trimms, Matt watched them float away.

The fire rapidly consumed much of the ship, rendering the engine immobile. As passengers scrambled, there was a semblance of order when boarding the lifeboats. The affluent were given priority. Matt, having a lower cabin assignment, was among the last to board. As his lifeboat was being lowered, a massive wave hit, tossing many passengers into the sea. The assigned crew managed to stabilize the boat in the middle of the Atlantic.

Rescue boats and nearby coastal ships received the distress call and promptly started the search. Five lifeboats in total drifted in the dark, with the Trimm's lifeboat being the first to be located and rescued. Gradually, all survivors were saved and provided with essentials.

A week later, they docked in Southampton. A designated facility awaited them, allowing survivors to reconnect with any separated loved ones. Announcements called out names, but when "Allan Brightman" echoed through the room, there was silence. The same went for the children, renamed Mark and Liam. Unaware of their new identities, and still mourning, the boys cried out for familiar comforts. By the end of the roll call, it was apparent: Matt had been lost to the storm.

Lady Trimm, heartbroken over the children's uncertain future, offered to take them in. However, it was decided they'd be placed in a government foster home. Now named Liam and Mark, the boys finally had stability.

Newspapers worldwide reported the maritime tragedy. Initially, reports indicated that all families had been informed about their loved ones' fate. As weeks passed, appeals for Allan Brightman's relatives grew more frequent. Overwhelmed by her own problems, Marie barely glanced at newspapers. Grief consumed her, making even daily tasks a challenge. Friends and family tried to offer support as best they could. Bills accumulated, and with Mr. Murray gone, Marie formed her own theories. She suspected Mr. Murray and Matt, whom she believed had undergone gender transitions, had taken the boys. This theory was strengthened by Mr. Murray's sudden disappearance and suspicions about the authenticity of his name.

Marie took on the role as operator of the Dress and Alterations shop but soon decided that the memories were too great. She let the shop go into bankruptcy and started her own little side business of alterations. She rented a spot in the neighborhood, and one of the ladies from the alteration shop came with her to help get started. Business was good, better than expected.

Time went on and the healing process of losing her babies weighed heavily on her heart. The Police were baffled, and the case was labeled as unsolved. Days turned into weeks, weeks into months, and several years passed. Marie became the owner of Marie's Alterations. There was no time for Marie to design, but she remade old fashions into new attire as times were tough and money was scarce.

Marie befriended a local café owner, Thomas, who had recently lost his wife to cancer. They were a comfort to each other and began to date. Thomas invited Marie on a three-night trip to New York for business, and she accompanied him. In New York, Marie visited museums and Central Park. It was in the park that she found a newspaper.

As she read it while waiting for Thomas, she stumbled upon a photo of Mark and Liam with the headline: "Orphaned Boys to be Adopted." Marie gasped. "My boys," she whispered, nearly fainting at the sight. When Thomas returned, they scoured the paper for the entire article and quickly contacted the journalist.

Weeks later, the newspaper sent Marie all the articles they had on the boys. She approached the police, who reopened the kidnapping investigation. Clues led them to the local shipyard where a Mr. Brightman was seen boarding a ship to Southampton. But the traces of Mr. Brightman were inconclusive; he was found dead at sea, near the remnants of a ship fire. It was ruled an accident. The passport was later found in a Southampton police department's box of unsolved crimes and was determined to be fake. DNA tests on the official papers revealed a shocking truth: Mr. Brightman was not Mr. Brightman.

The missing persons case evolved dramatically. Marie, accompanied by the lead investigator, flew to Southampton. She was taken to the Trimm home to potentially reunite with her boys. Carrying Luca's cherished toy chicken, she hoped for a sign of recognition. When the boys were brought out, older than she remembered, both reacted instantly. Marco, tears streaming down his face, ran to her, while Luca cried out, "My chicken!" and took the toy from Marie. Everyone present was convinced: these were Marie's boys. The Trimm family welcomed Marie into their home while she and the boys reacquainted. After handling extensive paperwork, the three of them flew back to Chicago.

Back home, with the help of her mom, Marie reintegrated the boys into their old life using belongings that had been stored. The police informed her that Mr. Murray was apprehended and was, in fact, Dave Snider, a criminal with a long rap sheet, including falsifying passports and stealing company records. Brought back to Chicago for trial, Marie never wanted to lay eyes on him again. The mystery of Matt's motivations for kidnapping the boys remained, but Marie hoped the boys wouldn't remember the ordeal. Now, with Thomas in their lives, Marie, Luca, and Marco had all the love they needed for a lifetime.

A TIME TO REMEMBER

Chapter One
As It Was…

The flat prairies and the distant mountains were drifting by the window. Polly was reflecting on her past life. Strangely enough, as she was thinking to herself, you meet the "perfect" man, and you get married. Marshall was just that man. Yet, was Polly's life anything but perfect? "Perfect never exists," Polly sighs.

Growing up on the farm with six—yes, all seven including me—brothers and sisters was not an easy life for Mom and Dad. Verona (Mom) and John (Dad) had come from Eastern Europe in the 1800s, and life on the old homestead was proving to be hard work with many labor-intensive times. Not speaking the English language, they found they had a community of foreigners to be their friends. Having your own land and animals had its advantages: milk, meat, eggs, chickens, and vegetables. Everyone had a job, whether it was raking the hay, planting the potatoes, hoeing the garden, getting meals prepared, or just looking after the younger children. Everyone had a task to perform. The girls were given hand-me-downs, and if you got a pair of your brother's trousers, you wore them.

The oldest children went to school when they could. Usually on horseback in twos, riding bareback there and back, or they would walk. Learning to read and write was a necessity if the day permitted it. You often couldn't go, as chores on the farm kept you home or a blinding snow blizzard made for poor attendance. Taught by one teacher in a one-room schoolhouse from grades one through nine, the boys were responsible for the wood in the old stove, and the girls cleaned the brushes. Recesses were the most fun; tag in the trees was the best. Often on a summer day, school was held outdoors as it was far too hot in the old schoolhouse. Once home, there were still cows to be milked and animals to be fed. "Wasn't it great?" recalled Polly. Back in the house, three bedrooms, with three boys in one room and four girls in the other. If there had been a baby, it always slept with Mom and Dad in their room. Share and share alike, the old saying went. You just learned to get along!

Chapter Two
In The Swing Of Things...

Parties, weddings, and funerals were always in the house. Having a party in your home, the whole family and even some townsfolk came. If you came by horse and carriage, you were lucky and got to stay the night. If you came by car, you brought others along with you. Furniture was moved outdoors to make way for dancing. Everyone chipped in and cooked the meal; there was always more than enough to go around and leftovers for the next day.

The local town of "Burmis" was where it all began. Today, all that is left of the town is a hill of grass; the stables, garages, and barns have all been taken down. Where the Old Church used to be is now a small knoll with rocks protruding on top. The old Church, which was heated by a wood-burning stove, saw many baptisms and weddings. If it was a good day, funerals were held there too.

"Father Joe" not only welcomed you to the Lord's House, but he was also always welcome in everyone else's home. Come Easter or Christmas, he came and blessed the homes, sharing a meal with the family and often breaking open a keg of beer for good luck.

Parties on the farm were just that: parties. Everyone came, smiling, laughing, and having fun. Music was always by a local group, and today was no exception. "Marshall" and his boys were playing tonight. Marshall was multi-talented, playing the harmonica, banjo, and piano. Another fellow played the accordion, and one man was a singer, toe-tapper, and yodeler. Marshall was tall, slim, with a full head of hair and a smile that would melt one's heart, and he was a fantastic dancer.

Polly, who grew up having very little, always wanted a dolly of her own but never had enough money to get one. Rations were thin, and a new pair of shoes might be an option if you were lucky. By age sixteen, she was all grown up, along with her two cousins, Kay and Veronica. They headed to the big city. An advertisement in the store mentioned that people were looking for chambermaids. They got the job at a rich farmer's place with lots of kids; the girls worked as Monday-to-Friday chambermaids. Often on a Friday, they would head into the big city and spend their money on hats, shoes, and cigarettes. That's where Marshall came in handy; with his car, he would take the girls wherever they wanted to go.

Chapter Three
Marshall

Marshall was a small-town lad from Coleman, a nearby mining town. He was raised by his father, John, and a stepmother, Charlotte, who was of German nationality. "Learn the language or go without," she said. Being the youngest, Marshall had a brother, Ludvik, and a sister, Anna. Their mother, Teresa, had been walking one winter's night, likely along the train tracks into the town. It was a blizzard, no doubt. She was the head of the Ladies Red Cross, and as one gets closer to town with the wind whipping around the tracks and the mine working 24/7, the noise is deafening. Teresa did not hear the train blowing its whistle. As tragic as the incident was, life went on. It was rumored that John had a lady friend, Charlotte, who had three children. She soon became the mother in the blended family.

Because Coleman was a mining town, it didn't mean that everyone worked in the mine. John owned his own meat market and butcher shop, with stables and cutting sheds in the back. He was well-known among the locals. If he wasn't working as a butcher, many believed he was a "Rum Runner," or, as it's known today, a bootlegger, which was, of course, illegal. The Mounties never caught him!

As the years went by, Marshall and all the other children grew up. Charlotte's three children eventually left home. Ludvik decided to visit California to see life there. In Buena, California, he met a young lady named Marlene. They married and together opened a dress shop in Buena. Ludvik was the salesman, and Marlene managed the store. The most expensive dress was priced at $2.95 during wartime. Hard times pressed on, and Ludvik took a second job delivering milk. One morning at 4:00 am, a drunk driver crashed into his milk truck, tragically ending Ludvik's life. The family faced another heartbreak.

Anna stayed behind, becoming the bookkeeper for her father's market. She learned all about financial prudence until she met a visiting Scottish lad in Cole. He won her heart and took her to Trail to be his wife, where they lived happily in the mining community.

The Marshall Band was a popular name in Cole, performing at local beer parlors and lake dances. Polly and Marshall were always the center of attention at these events. On March 2, 1945, they wed in the Cole Church. Though they couldn't afford photographs, they held a modest reception for the family. They lived above the meat market, making do with wooden crates for furniture.

Chapter Four
Life Goes On

Life on the farm progressed smoothly. A wonderful man named Martin immigrated from Europe and arrived by train in the Burmis area. Polly's father welcomed Martin and offered his daughter, Sophia's, hand in marriage. Sophia was young, but one didn't typically question their parents. Besides, Dad needed the money for his farm. Times were tough for everyone those days. The two were married in the Burm Church, hoping for a happy future.

Michael continued living on the farm in an old log cabin with his wife and son. There, they worked the land, paving the way for Michael's own farmstead.

Other siblings moved to nearby towns after marrying. Many became miners' wives.

Polly and Marshall became part of this community, with Marshall working in the mines. A miner's wife always knew the rhythm of the mines – when they were operational and when they were not. They could tell when it was safe to hang laundry outside without the soot from the mines tarnishing their clothes or when they could open their windows for a whiff of fresh air free from the scent of burning coal.

Working in the underground mine was lucrative but perilous. Every family was all too aware of the dangers but was always grateful when their loved ones returned home safely.

With the onset of challenging times and a looming war overseas, men were conscripted to serve. Marshall was on the "Reserve" list but contributed to his country by joining the Canadian Armed Forces Army Band. Though not the largest band member, he carried the tuba with pride. The band participated in many parades honoring army veterans. Marshall lived part-time in Red Deer and part-time in Coleman, but he and Polly kept their marriage strong. They bought their first home in Cole, a rarity with indoor plumbing. They even purchased a new car, a 1939 Chevrolet. Polly learned to drive when Marshall was away, sneaking in lessons and trips to Bingo without ever getting caught for driving without a license. Each time she returned safely, she breathed a "Sigh of Relief".

Chapter Five
Moving On With Life

Marshall's dad, John, and his wife, Charlotte, decided it was time to retire. The stables, outbuildings, and the land, which was home to the Meat Market all these years, were no longer theirs. They retired to a warmer climate: Grand Forks, BC. The meat market was still there, sold to a local resident.

Everyone was having children, but not for Polly and Marshall. Back in the day, you could adopt children through the Government. When children came up for adoption, the applicants that were accepted were notified a child was now available. No choice was given as to boy or girl.

In one of the Northern Cities, such a thing was happening. A couple, who would have made a wonderful family under different circumstances, had a baby girl. She was loved by her mom and dad but could not be part of their lives. This little girl was starting a new journey of her life. Polly and Marshall really did want a baby boy to carry on the family name. But, under this law, it was a take-it-or-leave-it decision. The little girl came home with Polly and Marshall. She fit into their lives quite nicely.

"Welcome Home," said Marshall. "Baby girl, you will be loved and spoiled by so many around you."

Even the baby book was in blue. Would that make a difference? Would anyone care?

As the road narrowed and the mountains became only visible in one's mind, sleep overcame Polly. While she rested, her mind recalled many wonderful days, both happy and sad.

Polly was in fitful sleep. John, her dad, had passed away at a very early age. Hard work and labor had taken his youth, leaving behind a widow and a small boy to look after the farmstead. Just when you think the impossible, a ray of sunshine happened. One day, a vagrant man came to the farmhouse door and asked if there was any work for him. He was trying to survive, willing to work for food and a bed, even if it was in the barn with the animals. Polly, Mom, Veroni, and her youngest son, Tomas, agreed to let the man work on the land and help with chores. In exchange, he could stay in the log cabin, now sitting vacant. This man, his name was Emru. Emru worked hard and long, and Veroni often made his meals, sending them to the cabin for him to enjoy. Emru lived on the family farm for many years. When he wanted to retire, the family could not send him away. Emru passed away on this farm, and the family gave him a proper burial.

"No man should have to die and be alone" was their custom.

Chapter Six
Life Of Polly

"Sigh," mumbled Polly as she was in the deepest of sleep. The wrinkles on her forehead showed her despair, reflecting the unpleasantness of her dreams. The baby had come to live with Polly and Marshall, but "what shall we name her?"

"Let us call her Margaret," said Polly. "Yes, she is a plump little girl with rosy cheeks and hazel eyes… yes, she is a Margaret."

Polly was quite the seamstress. She always made her own clothes and little dresses for Margaret. Sometimes dresses were repurposed from Polly's older dresses, and sometimes they had matching dresses. Margaret never had any siblings but made up for it with friends and cousins she could spend time with.

The snow crunched beneath their feet. It was snowing ever so lightly, but the wind had picked up. The walk was long, and darkness was coming quickly on this January night. "You need to look pretty at a party, especially a birthday party," stated Polly. Margaret's dress was pale pink with paler little roses made with love from one of Polly's dresses.

"If you could only smell the love from these delicate roses," thought Polly. "You must look like a young lady."

Walking up the hill through the snow, Polly wondered, "What was I thinking?"

"The Greyhound bus will pick us up at the Service Station, as that is his designated stop," Polly told a sobbing Margaret, cold from the journey. Once at the Service Station, the mechanic, who was also the owner, removed Margaret's shoes and wrapped her tiny feet in his jacket, rubbing them to restore circulation. He did this until the Greyhound arrived. Several miles down the road, the Greyhound stopped along the Highway at her aunt's home to let them off. By now, Margaret had stopped crying, knowing she would have fun with her cousin. The blizzard intensified, but all was well. Marshall was working the evening shift and couldn't drive them to their cousins, but he would have the day off tomorrow and would come for them by car. Polly and Margaret were to have a sleepover.

Marshall left his job at the Coal mine. His health was deteriorating, and per the doctor's advice, he needed to find alternative indoor work. Although still a young man, Marshall moved to the city and secured a job as a forklift operator. He lived with a friend, coming home some weekends. After six months, Marshall sent for his family to join him. Selling their home was heart-wrenching. Leaving friends and family behind and uprooting their lives was tough, but, as everyone said, "It's for the best."

All secrets could be deadly. Reliving her past, Polly comes to terms with her past life.

Being married for all the wrong reasons. As the dark clouds hang over me, there is no escape. There were so many before Marshall, but Marshall really did sweep me off my feet. "I have to get married," Polly thinks. That is NOT a good reason to marry. Not wanting to be left in the cold, Polly marries Marshall. It's a small church wedding; there are no photographs to share. The Catholic Church blesses the happy couple. After several months, the pregnancy was no longer. "How do I tell him what I have done?" she worries. "Why now?" she says out loud. I have paid the ultimate price, and I can't have children.

The worst part was that I treated Marshall as if this was his fault. He was never to blame, and he could never understand why I blamed him. When you have a daughter, you want to protect her, not wanting her to make the same mistakes that you made. Protection is one thing, but control is worse. Being jealous of Margaret, I shamed her into "my way." Shame caused so much friction. "Daughters can cause so much trouble and heartache," Polly often thought. She never gave Margaret a chance to live a normal childhood or to have a "father figure" in her life. All Polly saw were her own mistakes. She couldn't wait for her daughter to leave the home, thinking that would make all her memories go away.

Your past is just a story. Until you let it go, it will always have power over you. Silence is always full of answers.

Chapter Seven
Looking Back...

By this time, Marshall was getting weaker. Struggling for air was getting harder. He no longer wanted to be in this world of heartache and pain. When you lose a spouse, you tend to reach out to your roots. However, you soon realize that times change, people change, and move on; things are never as they were. You start over...

Blinking back the tears, Polly's mind whirls. The sun has set now, but you never give up. "You can pick your friends but not your relatives," Polly thinks to herself. Polly was definitely a friend to all and a good friend she was. People began to take advantage of her and her lifestyle. Polly and Marshall scrimped and saved for their retirement years, so Polly faced no hardship. Always remembering the hardships she faced on the farm and living with wooden crates for furniture, Polly loved new and expensive things. Sewing was a thing of the past, and she was a great dresser. Travelling frequently, often alone, she enjoyed the life she had left. You have heard of people scamming others. Well, it happens to those you care about, only the scammers are people you used to love.

Margaret was a devoted, caring daughter regardless of the past between her and her mom. She knew no other way than to love those close to her. Margaret thought, "Isn't that how all children are treated? All families are dysfunctional, aren't they?"

Time goes by, and life changes you forever. Lacking the strength to carry on, Polly succumbed to health issues at 87. Polly remained the beautiful, fair-skinned lady she had been in her younger years, only age had taken its toll on her.

She suffered from a terrible disease: Alzheimer's and Dementia. Living with memories of being a child, unable to read properly, and reading upside-down newspapers were the first giveaway signs. "Tie your bonnet, Anna," "Tomas, you're a bad boy," "Veroni, you're hurting me," she'd say. She would ask Margaret how she arrived, but Margaret was not far away in years; Polly was way back, not current at all. Hearing your mother ask to be taken home is one of the hardest things to hear. Life, on the other side, is childish, unreal, and confusing for everyone.

How does one cope? The answer is simple: One day at a time. One minute at a time. Go with the flow. You have an impaired ability to think; your decisions are masked. It often comes with a price... This is how it will end, as a shrieking tea kettle comes to a boil and subsides.

Beautiful things aren't just objects, people, places, memories, or pictures. Beauty lies in the feelings, the moments, the smiles, and the laughter we share. Polly is awake, and her subconscious is at peace. Peace, I bring to each and every one.

Made in United States
Troutdale, OR
12/29/2023

16540704R00075